MINE

By J. Kahele

Book Cover designed by Nate Garcia

My mind wanders to the dark place — the place only I can go

— J. Kahele

Table of Contents

Chapter I 4

Chapter II 33

Chapter III 68

Chapter IV 100

Chapter V 129

Chapter VI 162

Chapter VII 194

Chapter VIII 228

Chapter IX 257

Chapter X 283

Chapter I

The alarm ringing awakens me from my slumber. I tap my phone, silencing it, curling to my pillow for an extra few minutes of sleep. My husband Ben, ruffling the bed as he plops on it, forces my eyes open. I turn to face him with a smile.

"There's my beautiful girl." He murmurs as he caresses my cheek softly. I close my eyes, embracing his touch.

"Good morning."

"Good morning, darling. I was hoping you could help me out, I sort of over-scheduled myself again." I sit up and he places his hand in mine, fiddling with my fingers.

"What do you need me to do?" He reaches for a stack of papers from the night stand.

"I need this paperwork dropped off today to the attorney's office."

"I thought our attorney was in New York?"

"William opened a firm here, and his son Andrew is running it. It would help me out tremendously if you could drop the paperwork off for me. I would do it, but I have an important meeting in just fifteen minutes that I cannot be late for." He explains, staring at his watch.

"Of course I'll do it." He embraces me tightly.

"Thank you darling. Remember I'm flying to New Hampshire tonight, I won't be returning till late tomorrow."

"I remember. Have a safe flight."

"I really have to run. I love you." He kisses me quickly and stands.

"I love you too." I respond. He smiles; stroking my hair softly, then leaves.

I remember the first time I laid eyes on Ben. I was employed at a dental office as a part time receptionist, when he strolled up to my desk to check in for his appointment.

His wavy, flaxen hair and alluring, chestnut eyes were a perfect mix, an attraction developed between us instantly.

"Hi, I am Benjamin Kramer; I am here to see Dr. Caran." He announces, with a flawless grin.

The mature nature and polite pronunciation of his words made me nervous. I could see right away he was an intelligent and confident man. My mind stumbles as I type on the computer, and his last name leaves me. I sit, tapping the keyboard, attempting to remember, but it is to no avail as my juvenile brain was not cooperating. I swallow hard and exhale lightly.

"I'm sorry. I, uh, forgot your last name." I tell him, stuttering.

"Kramer." He replies with a light-hearted chuckle. I exhale with relief as I enter his name in the appointment book.

"I apologize for the delay, Mr. Kramer; someone will be out to get you in a few minutes."

"Thank you. And your name is?"

"Jenna Dotson." I stutter.

"You are new here."

"I just started two days ago." He nods his head.

"So, how do you like working here?"

"I have only worked here for two days, so I don't even know yet." I respond with a light giggle.

"Oh Yes. I can understand that." The hygienist opens the door and calls his name. He turns to me with a big smile.

"It was a pleasure to meet you, Jenna."

"It was nice to meet you, Mr. Kramer." He nods his head, and walks to the hygienist.

As the clocks hit 8:00, I shut down my computer and stand up, grasping my coat from behind my chair. I walk out of the office, and immediately notice a long black stretched limo. As I pass it, the door opens, and Benjamin Kramer steps out.

"Good Evening, Jenna."

"Good Evening, Mr. Kramer."

"Please, call me Ben."

"Ben."

"What are your plans this evening?"

"I was just going to go home and relax."

"I would really like to take you to dinner, that is, if you would like to go?" He says sweetly.

His comment astounds me; a good looking, powerful, and rich man wanting to take me to dinner. The first question in my mind is why?

"Why would you want to take me to dinner?" I ask him suspiciously.

"Why wouldn't I?"

"Because, I'm only a 17 year old high school student, and you are a Senator."

"I am asking to take you to dinner Jenna, not to bed you. I assure you it is totally platonic."

"I don't know. My brother in law wouldn't be happy about me taking off with a strange man."

"I am not a strange man. I am a Senator, a friend of the people. I assure you I will keep my hands firmly in these pockets." He places his hands in his pants pockets. I stare up at him and he has a childlike expression on his face, like I was a toy he wanted so badly, but couldn't have. It brings a smile to my face.

"Ok, but my curfew is ten on a school night." I say to him. He exhales, and a grin encompasses his face.

"I will make sure you are home by then." He opens the door of the limo and I step in, and he slides in beside me.

From that day forward, we were never separated. Ben showered me with lavish gifts, late night dinners, and romantic walks down the beach. He literally swept me off of my feet.

Ben's want and need to be with me was a little overwhelming, and he became instantly overprotective, needing to know every second of the day where I was.

We were together every day and sometimes all night. But it was never enough for Ben; he was persistent in having me with him always. Within a few months, we were married.

As the memory leaves me, I exhale, stepping out of bed, strolling to the bathroom to shower. I turn on the bathroom DVD player and press number 6.

The warm water revitalizes me as it streams down my body. The hot steam tantalizes my skin, invigorating me. Van Morrison's "Into the Mystic" blares through the bathroom.

As I rinse my hair, I sing loudly to the song. I shut the shower off and wrap myself comfortably in a towel and walk back to the bedroom. I gaze at the clock, and realize I had taken longer than I should have to shower. I rush to my closet and gaze quickly through my wardrobe. I spot a grey linen skirt suit and a white button up top. I pull it from the hanger and dress quickly. I walk to the bathroom and hurriedly put my hair up. I finish my makeup and grasp the stack of papers and my purse and walk out to the kitchen.

Helda, our housekeeper, approaches me immediately.

"Mrs. Kramer, can I get you anything?" she asks me.

"Just coffee, thank you." I gaze over the very large stack of papers for the attorneys. I look through the first few and notice it is a list of homes we own.

A shadow above me interrupts my concentration. I stare up, and Rocco is standing over me.

"Excuse me, Mrs. Kramer." I stand straight up and turn to Rocco. "Belis wants to know when you were planning on leaving for the attorney's office." Rocco asks pleasantly.

Belis was our limo driver, an immigrant from Russia. His English was very staggered and sometimes incomprehensible. Rocco was fluent in Russian, being born to Russian parents, so he often interpreted for Belis.

"About ten minutes." I answer quickly.

"Ok ma'am I will let him know." Rocco smiles and leaves the room. Rocco is one of many assigned body guards of Ben's. Whenever I went anywhere besides work, Rocco went with me.

I place my coffee mug gently in the sink. Then walk over to the table, grasping my purse and the attorney papers, I then stroll out the door to the limo. Belis stands by the open door, I step inside and he closes the door. He backs out of the driveway, and we are on our way, our destination: Carington Associates.

Within fifteen minutes, the limo pulls ups to a large tan brick building. Belis opens my door. I step out and stare up at the words, "Carington Associates" that encompassed the middle of the building in large, burgundy letters. I stroll up to the glass that encased the front of the building. Rocco opens the door for me, and I walk in.

The lobby is open, with cathedral ceilings and recess lighting throughout. The walls are painted with a shiny white paint. Green and burgundy crown molding splits the walls in half.

A circular, round, white desk sits in the middle of the black marble floors. A sign above it reads "Information". Rocco and I walk over to it. A small woman in her early twenties with choppy short red hair and dark blue eyes smiles at me as I stand before her.

"Can I help you?" the woman asks me, pleasantly. I stare down at the paperwork for the attorney's name.

"Yes. I'm here to see Andrew Carington." I answer politely.

"Your name?"

"Jenna Kramer." I tell her.

"I will let Mr. Carington know you are here, ma'am. You can have a seat over there." she tells me, pointing to a sitting area with white leather couches, and dark Berber carpet. I nod my head, and walk over to the sitting area. Rocco sits down next to me.

"When I go in, you can stay out here." I tell Rocco. He shakes his head.

"The Senator said where you go, I go." Rocco retorts. Rocco was a very large man at 6'4", 350 lbs. He feared Ben, so I would often take that into consideration when he would disregard my requests.

"Rocco, do not fight me on this. I assure you nothing is going to happen to me in the attorney's office. You can stay out here." I tell him sternly. Apprehensively, he nods his head.

The red-haired woman walks over to me.

"Mr. Carington will see you now. Please follow me." she says with a smile. I stand, and so does Rocco. I turn to him.

"Stay here Rocco." I tell him strongly. He exhales and plops down on the couch, pouting. I giggle at his reaction.

The hallway is in the same décor as the lobby. As we walk to the end, she knocks lightly on a frosted glass door, and then cracks it open.

"Mr. Carington, Jenna Kramer." she says.

"Show her in, Jill." the voice answers. She opens the door widely.

"Please go in." she says to me, still smiling. I walk into the office. It is spacious, decorated in a dark cherry wood. A sitting area is situated to the left of the room with a bar, large entertainment center, and two dark brown leather couches.

A matching dark cherry wood desk is centered perfectly in front of a glass encompassed wall. A man sits in a high-back black leather chair, tilted back, talking on the phone with his back facing me. As I walk closer to his desk, he turns, hanging up the phone, and faces me. I am taken back as I look at him. He stands, and the song "I Want to Kiss you all over" instantly floods my mind.

He is beautiful and tall, at about 6'1". With short brown, nicely groomed hair and piercing blue eyes. His teeth are white as the snowfall, and his hands, perfectly manicured; he is wearing a navy suit, light navy shirt, all fitted just right to show off his muscular stature. He looks up at me with a half-lipped, sexy smile.

"Mrs. Kramer?" He says pleasantly. Even his voice is appealing, soft, and sultry, causing a light exhale from my mouth. I shake my head, regaining my composure.

"Yes… I'm Mrs. Kramer." I respond to him.

"I am Andrew Carington. Please, have a seat." he says to me gesturing to a chair in front of his desk. I gently sit on the chair and he follows suit. I hold the papers in my hand.

"Are those for me?" He asks, still smiling, pointing to the papers in my hand. I nod my head.

"Yes." I respond, handing him the papers.

He gazes through them with a pen in his hand. I can't help but stare at him; he is so beautiful. He tilts his eyes, looking up at me.

"You don't look old enough to be a Senator's wife." he says out of the blue. I am a little shocked by his statement.

"Excuse me?" I murmur softly.

"I don't believe I was speaking in a foreign tongue." he responds with sarcasm. Appalled by his comment, I sit forward.

"Your comment is very offensive, Mr. Carington." I tell him abruptly.

"My apologies, Mrs. Kramer. If I offended you, it was not meant to be offensive. Just an honest opinion." he says calmly. I sit back on the chair. His comment still lingers in my mind, causing me to frown. He looks up at me and smiles.

"I have really upset you haven't I?"

"No, I'm fine." I answer quickly. He places his pen and the papers down on the desk.

"I think I have everything I need." he says, folding his hands and sitting forward.

"Good." I stand back up.

"Mrs. Kramer do you have ants in your pants?" he asks me with a chuckle.

"Mr. Carington why is it that you find it necessary to be so bold with me?" I ask him.

"Bold? Well I don't believe I was being bold Mrs. Kramer. I was just having a conversation." Not wanting to pursue the conversation any further, I nod my head.

"Mr. Carington I am in a rush, if you need nothing further from me, I would like to go."

"You are free to go, after you tell me how old you are." he says with a smile.

"Why is my age so important to you?" I ask him with irritation.

"Why is hiding your age so important to you?" he responds as he picks up a pen, tapping it on the desk. His eyes never leave mine; he stares at me, awaiting an answer. He places his leg over his knee and leans back on his chair, sliding the pen across his lip slowly. His gesture arouses me. I never wanted to be a pen so badly in my life. I swallow hard then answer.

"I'm 22." I sit back down on the chair.

"I was right; you are far too young to be a Senator's wife… You had to be quite young when you married. How old were you when you married?" he asks me.

"More questions, what does my age or marriage have to do with the paperwork I have given you?" I ask him with frustration.

"Absolutely nothing, I am just making conversation." I exhale and sit back down.

"I was 18."

"I am correct again, you were barely out of high school when you married… way too young." He preaches proudly.

"Actually, I was a senior in high school. I married Ben in March, and graduated that June." I retort. He shakes his head.

"Why would your parents allow you to marry so young?" he asks me. I exhale.

"I was raised by my sister and brother in law. Ben and I eloped marrying without their knowledge."

"They must have been quite upset by your decision. I know that I would have not been too happy if my sister had run off and married so young."

"They were not happy about it."

"Senator Kramer has to be in his 30's at least."

"He is 39." I tell him.

"That is quite an age difference."

"Love has no age limitations, Mr. Carington."

"Touché, Mrs. Kramer." Andrew says with a grin. He lightly bites his bottom lip, and I can feel my mouth go dry.

"Do you have any siblings, Mr. Carington?"

"No. I am an only child."

"Oh, that explains why you are the way you are."

"The way I am? I don't quite understand, Mrs. Kramer."

"You are the most judgmental man I have ever met." I respond rudely. He laughs at my comment.

"You have been able to come to that conclusion in just this short conversation we have had?" he asks, grinning.

"Yes."

"Well, Mrs. Kramer, I also am very self centered and selfish." He responds proudly. I shake my head. He reaches to his business card holder situated in the corner of his desk, retrieving one from it.

"Here is my card, call me if you have any questions." He says to me as he places it in front of me. I pick up the card and place it in my purse.

"Thank you."

"It has my personal cell phone number on it. Please use it if you need it. I make myself available 24/7 to all my clients." He says with a wicked grin.

I stand once again.

"Thank you for your time, but I really must go." I tell him sternly.

"Of course, please inform your husband that I will have the paperwork ready for him by the earlier part of next week." He bends his head, and again starts reading through the papers in front of him. I turn and walk away, as I reach the door, he stops me.

"Mrs. Kramer." he shouts. I turn around and walk back over to his desk.

"You have a wonderful day." he says with a smile. I exhale with frustration and stomp away.

"Arrogant son of a bitch!" I murmur to myself as I stomp out of the building.

As we drive down the road, I retrieve my cell and his card and key his number into my cell. I instruct the driver to drive me back to my house so I could retrieve my vehicle. I despised being driven, especially to work.

My office is located in a restored Victorian house from the 1800's. It has three floors, and had been renovated with 50 small offices.

The bottom floor has a modern kitchen with stainless steel appliances, granite countertops, and a large conference room. I rush up to my office and begin my day.

Whenever Ben was out of town, I would make plans with my sister, Christie, it was the only time I was able to break free and enjoy myself. We make plans to meet at a local pub for dinner and drinks. I then call Ben. He answers on the first ring.

"Hello Darling." Ben answers immediately.

"Hi. How is your day so far?" I ask him pleasantly.

"Better now that you called." He responds sweetly. Ben was very overprotective of me, so I always became nervous when I would have to ask him to go anywhere.

"I'm calling because I was wondering if you would be okay with me going out with Christie tonight." I ask him nervously. He pauses for a moment, and I can tell he is pondering my question in his head.

"Is it just you and Christie going?" he asks me.

"Yes."

"I don't know, Jenna, two women alone…" He says apprehensively.

"It's just dinner." I tell him. He exhales loudly. "Between our jobs and my schedule, I hardly ever get to see my sister." I plead.

"Will you be drinking?" he asks.

"A few drinks, that's all."

"Well if I allow you to go, you have to promise that you will not drink and drive, and check in with me as soon as you are home. If you can assure me that you can do these two things I ask, then I suppose I see no harm in you going." Ben explains to me.

"Thank you." I respond with excitement. Ben chuckles.

"Anything to make you happy." He responds.

"It made me very happy." I tell him smiling.

"Ok darling, I do have to go. Call me when you get in."

"Ok. Bye."

"Wait." He says quickly.

"What is it?"

"I love you?" he asks in a childlike manner. I chuckle.

"I love you." I respond happily.

"I love you too. Have a good day."

The day flies by, and before I know it, I am driving to the pub to meet Christie. I walk into the pub and gaze around for her. She waves her hand, catching my attention, and I walk over to the table. She stands, hugging me.

"I can't stay long. I have a meeting early in the morning." She states firmly.

Christie was a social worker who mainly worked with the elderly. We both sit down, and I pick up a menu, gazing at it.

"Jenna, dad called me last night." Christie says as she gazes across the menu. I place my menu down and look up at her.

"Where is he at now?" I ask her.

"Poland." She responds immediately. I shake my head.

I had lost my mother when I was only 12 years old to cancer. My father was so distraught from my mother's death; he plummeted into a deep depression. He would leave for days at a time, and after a year, he finally just left us altogether. Christie was 18 and her boyfriend at the time, Manny, moved in and helped with the bills. Christie and Manny married when I was 14 years old, and Manny became protective of me instantly.

Manny had no respect for Ben, he often called him a pedophile for his attraction to me at such a young age. He was devastated when he learned I had run off and married Ben. To this day he blames the desertion of my father for the reason I married Ben.

"I miss daddy, Christie." I tell her sadly.

"I know I miss him too." She responds, hugging me. We sit, chatting, and have a few drinks, and then leave.

I drive home, thinking of my parents. I drive up in the driveway and the garage door opens, and out walks Rocco. He opens my door for me, and we walk into the house. I place my purse on the dining room table.

"The Senator wants you to give him a call." Rocco says to me. I nod, and retrieve my cell from my purse, calling Ben. He answers on the first ring.

"Hello darling." Ben answers.

"Hi." I respond to him.

"Did you just get home?" he asks me.

"Yes."

"Did you have a good time with your sister?"

"Yes. My father called her today."

"Oh. Where is he?"

"Poland." I tell him. I exhale.

"You miss him." he says softly.

"I do, a lot."

"Your father made his own choices, do not grieve for him… I miss you so much Jenna, being away from you is getting harder and harder." He says, distraught.

"I miss you too." I respond to him.

"It's late and you need to get your rest. I want you to take Rocco with you to work tomorrow. My flight comes in early, so I will come to your office and pick him up."

"Ok. Bye."

"Hey." He says quickly.

"Yes."

"I love you."

"I love you too. Goodnight." I respond. I hang my cell up, and walk into the bedroom, collapsing on the bed.

The light shining in through my window wakes me early. I stare at the clock, and it reads 5:00 a.m. I attempt to turn over and go back to sleep, but my eyes are wide awake. I decide to shower.

I finish showering, and walk into my closet to retrieve my outfit for the day. I spot a black leather skirt and pull it from the hanger too quickly, knocking over other hangers.

Clothes fall to the ground.

I bend, picking them up, and notice a pair of blue jeans amidst the pile. I grasp them in my hand and smile as I looked at them, not even realizing I still had them. Ben despised blue jeans; when we married he made me dispose of all that I had. I slide them on and smile.

I stroll out to the living room to watch the morning news after I am finished getting ready for work. Rocco is sitting in the living room, watching cartoons. I giggle and shake my head.

Helda prepares an English muffin and coffee for my breakfast. I eat the English muffin, tearing it apart into small pieces, then drink my coffee. I stand up, placing my cup and dish in the sink.

"Come on Rocco, it's time to go." I say to him. He stands up and walks into the kitchen.

"Are we taking the limo?" he asks me with concern.

"No. I never take the limo to work, you know that." A frightened look encompasses his face immediately. I pat him on the shoulder.

"You'll be alright." I tell him. We walk out to the car. Rocco steps into the passenger side as I step into the driver's side. After he latches his seat belt he does the sign of the cross and closes his eyes.

Rocco loathed driving with me. I was a very fast, impatient driver, and would change lanes quickly and often.

I was changing lanes and riding the bumper of the car in front of me as I gazed into the mirror, putting lipstick on.

"Mrs. Kramer, he's hitting his brakes!" Rocco screams frantically. I swerve into the next lane. I look over at Rocco, and his breathing is sparse.

"It's fine Rocco, I know how to drive." I tell him with a grin. He shakes his head and closes his eyes for the remainder of the ride. We drive into the parking lot of the office, and I turn the car off.

"Thank you Jesus." Rocco murmurs. I turn to him and laugh. We step out of the car and walk up to the office.

As I walk through the door I am immediately met by my boss, Kathleen.

"Good morning Jenna. What's he doing here?" Kathleen asks me as she looks at Rocco.

"Ben made me bring him' he's picking him up later." I tell her.

"Are you sure? Or is it that he's afraid that you may do something wrong at work." Kathleen says with aggravation. Kathleen was a very independent woman, and despised the way Ben hovered and overprotected me; she felt he was too smothering.

"I need to see you in my office. You can stay down here, Rocco." Kathleen tells him sternly.

"Where Mrs. Kramer goes, I have to go." He responds to Kathleen. She rolls her eyes at him.

"Oh alright, if you must come, then come." She tells him, shaking her head.

We follow her up the stairs to her office. She walks behind her desk, sitting down, and I sit in one of the chairs in front of her desk, Rocco sits in a chair in the corner.

"We decided to hire an outside attorney firm to handle the Busa lawsuit." she says to me.

"Why?" I ask her, confused.

"This lawsuit is more than our attorneys can handle. The Busa Company is a large organization, we have found that their attorneys are quite clever and more skilled than ours." she explains.

"So who did you hire?" I ask her with wonder.

"Carington Associates." she responds. I stare at her, astounded.

"Really?" I let out a chuckle as Andrew enters my mind.

"Why do you find that so humorous?" she asks me.

"No reason. They're our attorneys, also." I tell her.

"I know. Ben is the one who suggested them to us." she says to me.

Kathleen and her husband Franklin started the business shortly after they were married, off of one small account. Within 3 years, they had grown the business to a multi-million dollar enterprise. Ben and Franklin were best friends and had known each other since they were small children. He trusted Franklin completely. I was constantly complaining about not have nothing to do, so when a position came up with their company, Ben suggested me, and they hired me. Ben liked the idea of me working somewhere he could have control of. Franklin bowed down to Ben, and Ben would choose when I would work and when I wouldn't, without complaint from Franklin.

"Well, I'm happy for you. Are we finished? I have a lot of work to do." I say to her as I stand up.

"No… Sit back down." She says to me sternly. "You have been dealing closely with this lawsuit. I want you to work with the attorneys on this. They should be here any minute." She continues.

"I don't know." I tell her worriedly. Ben was a very jealous man, he wouldn't be happy about me working with men all day.

"I'm not asking." Kathleen responds sternly. I nod my head hesitantly.

The receptionist rings Kathleen's phone.

"Mrs. Carter, there is an Andrew Carington here to see you." The receptionist says to her. His name sends a sensation through my body.

"We will be right down, Kim." Kathleen responds.

Kathleen stands up and walks out of the office towards the stairs, and I follow. Andrew smirks as he sees me walking down the stairs with Kathleen.

"Well, Mrs. Kramer. I didn't know you worked here. It's a pleasure to see you again." Andrew says with a cocky smirk. I roll my eyes as his cocky smirk irritates me.

"Mr. Carington." I murmur blandly. He extends his hand out to Rocco.

"Andrew Carington." He says, shaking Rocco's hand.

"Rocco, I'm Mrs. Kramer's bodyguard." Rocco responds to him. Andrew laughs.

"Is this office so dangerous that you need a bodyguard?" Andrew asks jokingly.

"No, her husband is completely over the top." Kathleen responds with irritation. Andrew nods his head.

"You must be very important to him." Andrew says with a smile. I blush, looking down.

"Jenna will be working with you on the lawsuit. She is very familiar with the case and can give you all the reports and information you will need. We are giving you use of our conference room, we figured you would need a lot of room to work. If you follow me I will show you where it's at." Kathleen informs Andrew.

"Actually, Mrs. Carter, I have a few associates meeting me here, so I wanted to kind of wait around for them." Andrew tells her.

"Ok. I'm going to go back up to my office. Jenna will show you around." Kathleen says to Andrew. I shake my head nervously. Kathleen smiles at me, then walks to the stairs. Andrew walks up to me.

"Do you know where I can get a cup a coffee?" he asks nicely. I nod my head.

"Yes. I'll show you the kitchen." I respond. I walk towards the kitchen, standing near the fridge, and Andrew follows. I point towards the coffee pot.

"The receptionist makes a fresh pot every morning. There is powered creamer or liquid in the fridge. The coffee cups are in that cabinet." I tell him, pointing to the cabinet to the side of the sink.

"Thank you." he walks over to the cabinet and takes out a cup, then lifts the pot, pouring coffee into his cup. He then walks towards the fridge. Rocco immediately stops him as he gets closer to me. Andrew throws his hands in the air.

"I'm just getting the creamer." He tells Rocco slowly. Rocco nods his head and steps aside.

I move aside as he takes the creamer out, pouring it in his cup. While sipping his coffee, he tilts his eyes up at me, smiling.

"Very creamy." he says provocatively. I exhale.

Two men rush into through the front door and into the kitchen.

"Do you know who is out there?" the red haired man says with excitement to Andrew.

"Senator Kramer!" the dark haired man responds. The red haired man turns to the dark haired man.

"Matt. I wanted him to guess!" the red haired man says, perturbed.

"Sorry." Matt responds to him. Andrew chuckles.

"Eric and Matt this is Jenna"—Andrew is interrupted.

"Kramer." Ben says as he walks up to me. He wraps his arms around my waist, turning me to face him. He places his lips on mine, kissing me softly.

"Hello darling." he says with a smile. He looks me up and down, and a frown appears on his face as he sees the blue jeans. "We will talk about this in a minute." He whispers in my ear as he tugs on one of my belt loops. I nod my head.

He walks towards Andrew, extending his hand to him.

"Hello Andrew." Ben says, shaking his hand.

"Hello Senator." Andrew responds to him.

"How is your father, Andrew?" Ben asks Andrew.

"He is very well. Thank you for asking sir." Andrew responds.

"Your father is a good man… A very good man indeed." Ben states. Eric nudges Andrew.

"Senator Kramer, these are my associates, Eric Saley and Matt Cross." Andrew introduces. Ben shakes both of their hands.

"Andrew please, call me Ben… It's a pleasure to meet you both." Ben says to them. Ben turns to me.

"Darling can I talk to you for a moment, alone?" Ben asks me. I nod. He places his hand in mine, and walks me to the side.

"What on earth are you wearing? What have I told you about wearing blue jeans?" he asks quietly, with an angry stare.

"I am just at work." I respond instantly. My comment infuriates him' he grabs my wrists, pulling me to him too quickly, throwing me off balance. I slam my cheek on the wall.

"Ow!" I grimace as I grasp my cheek. Andrew and Eric rush over to us.

"Senator Kramer, take your hands off of her this instant!" Eric says to him madly. Ben exhales and releases me.

"I apologize for the disruption, it was a complete accident." Ben responds, smiling.

"It didn't look like an accident to me!" Eric states with irritation.

"It's okay, Eric." Andrew responds, attempting to calm him. Ben walks up to Eric, patting him on the shoulder.

"I am happy my wife will have you here to protect her." Ben tells him with a smile. He nods his head, but still glares at Ben.

Ben places his hand in mine and we walk to the front door.

"Come home directly after work." Ben says to me sternly.

"I will." I respond to him.

"I love you." He says as he kisses me quickly.

"I love you too." I murmur. He opens the door and leaves.

Andrew walks up to me, carrying an icepack. He stares at my cheek and gently places it on it.

"Ow!" I grimace as the coolness stings my aching cheek.

"Sorry… Is he always so hard-handed with you?" Andrew asks me worriedly.

"No. He didn't mean it, it was an accident." I tell him. He exhales and nods his head. I take the icepack from Andrew and place it on my cheek.

"Can you show us the way to the conference room?" Andrew asks me.

"Follow me." I tell them. I walk them down the hallway and to the conference room. Eric approaches me.

"You know I used to look up to your husband, until now. I don't have any respect for men who hit women." Eric tells me.

"It was an accident." I murmur.

"I don't think so." Eric responds. He walks over to the back of the room. I sit down, and start organizing the reports.

I found myself staring at Andrew throughout the day. There was something about the way his hair laid, the way his eyes smiled when he laughed.

I turn on the television in the conference room to watch the news. I walk back over to the stack of papers on the conference table and begin to organize them, when I hear Ben's name. I gaze up at the television, and see a picture of Ben walking hand in hand with a petite brunette. I walk over to the television, and, using the remote I turn the volume up on the television. The news reporter speaks:

"Senator Kramer is seen here with Senator Hillary Barker. Seems that these two Senators are getting awfully cozy..." Andrew takes the remote from me and turns off the television. I turn to him.

"Don't listen to that garbage. The media tells nothing but lies." Andrew says, shaking his head with disgust. He places the remote on the table. I walk back over to the stack of papers.

"So Jenna, does your husband travel often?" Eric asks me.

"Yes. He travels all the time."

"That has to be lonely." Eric responds.

"I'm used to it." He smiles at me, and I smile back.

I finish my last stack of reports, and place them on the table. I stare up at the conference room clock and its 5:30. Eric stands up, stretching.

"I'm starving, let's go eat." he says to Andrew.

"How about you, Jenna, are you hungry?" Andrew asks me.

"Thank you for the invitation, but I really need to get home." I tell him. He nods his head.

"Ok. See you tomorrow."

"Bye." I grasp my purse and leave.

Chapter II

I drive at top speed home, swerving in out of traffic to avoid the ever changing stop lights. I notice I am in the wrong lane, and was on the verge of missing my street. At the last minute, I swerve over, cutting a driver off, he honks his horn relentlessly, screaming obscenities out the window at me. I smile as I turn quickly on to my street.

I drive into the driveway and I am surprised to see Ben is already home. I open the garage and walk into the house. I am met by Ben immediately. He kisses me on the cheek.

"How was your day?" he asks pleasantly.

"It was exhausting." I tell him. He takes my hand and walks me over to the dining room table. Two plates are placed across from each other, filled with food.

"Come and eat, darling." He tells me. I nod and slide into my chair, Ben sits across from me. My plate included a small chicken breast, peas, and apple slices. A wine glass filled with red wine in front of it. Ben sits at the table across from me.

I cut up my chicken breast into small pieces and slowly eat it, chewing every piece until it practically evaporated in my mouth. Ben stares at me as I eat every morsel. After I finish my dinner, I drink my wine. Ben finishes and takes his plate and mine to the kitchen sink. Helda is cleaning the kitchen when Ben approaches her. He reaches into his pocket and hands her a list.

"I need you to go to the store and get everything on this list." He explains to her.

"Yes sir." Helda responds. She takes off her apron and leaves immediately. Ben walks over to the table and extends his hand to me.

I stand, taking his hand and we walk down the hall to the bedroom. I walk into the bedroom and stand near the end of the bed.

I hear the locking of the bedroom door and my body begins to tremble. Ben takes his suit jacket off, draping it over the chair. Loosening up his tie, he removes it, placing it atop his suit coat. He unbuttons the two top buttons of his shirt. He walks over to me, turning me to face him. He kisses me softly on the lips.

"You have been a very bad girl, haven't you?" he whispers creepily. I can feel the blood rush from my face.

"I'm sorry Ben." I respond, my heart beating quickly. He neatly rolls the sleeves of his shirt up.

"Undress… Now!" He tells me sternly. I quickly remove all my clothes till I'm standing naked before him.

"Please Ben, I promise I won't do it again!" I plead to him.

"I tire of your disobedience!" He says with frustration.

"I'm sorry, it won't happen again!" I tell him desperately.

"How can I believe a word you say, when you have defied me over and over again?" He asks with irritation. I look down to the ground.

I hear the all too familiar clatter of his gold-buckle, dark brown leather belt as he unbuckles it.

"Face the bed." He orders. I turn and face the bed.

"You took an oath to obey and honor me, till… death… do us part. You have disobeyed me again and now I must punish you!"

I stand, trembling, awaiting the punishment.

I feel the wind as he raises the belt in the air, and then, with merciless force, the belt strikes my lower back, savagely ripping my flesh.

He grips the belt tightly with his hand, raising it again.

The snap of the leather scorches my skin so viciously, my toes curl as it slams down on my lower back. My breath quickens, as his tortuous punishment continues.

He raises the belt again, aiming for the top of my thighs. He misses, hitting my side, causing me to flinch.

"Darling you moved, now we have to start all over again!" Ben says nonchalantly. I exhale and close my eyes tightly.

He raises the belt again. Without conscience or regret, he swings the belt into the air, then, with a deep fury, he slams it down on my back.

I tremble as the pain sears through me, but I don't scream. I never scream, I hold it inside. His relentless punishment continues until he tires. I stand completely still, my body trembling as tears fall down my face. Ben places his hands gently on my shoulders.

"Lie on the bed." he whispers in my ear. I crawl on my knees, lying on my stomach. Ben leaves the room. He returns fifteen minutes later.

"You are my wife, and you need to learn to obey me and what I say. I am only trying to help you."

He crawls in between my legs, and places cream on the bloody belt marks. I whimper as the cream burns. I realize it was the cream that Ben had sent Helda to the store for.

My mind wanders to the dark place, the place where only I can go.

I stare out aimlessly at the blank wall. Ben lies next to me, stroking my head gently.

The morning after was always the worse, the horrific memories of the night before quickly fills my mind as the bloody marks that encrusted my body throbbed painfully. Another emotional scar is added to the collection of pain and heartbreak I had endured over the years from Ben.

Ben walks over to the bed, rubbing cream on the bloody marks.

"I don't enjoy punishing you, but you need to learn to obey me. How you dress and present yourself reflects on me. I am a Senator, and I have an obligation to uphold a certain way of living, dressing, and presenting myself. You are my wife, so these rules apply to you also." Tears fall down my face.

"I'm sorry." I respond tearfully. He ignores my apology.

"I called you into work. I told them you had the flu. Make things easier on both of us and abide by the rules." he says to me.

I lay silently, as desolation overwhelms me, his words savagely tearing at my already severed heart. He kisses me on the forehead, and walks out of the room

My mind plummets into a dark hole. The reality of my existence enveloped me into a solitary desolation of hopelessness and agony. Ben left town that day. Whenever I would disobey Ben, he found it necessary to leave me alone to think and wallow in my misery. It was just another one of his dysfunctional ways of making me suffer. And it did. His lack of affection and compassion tore deep into my inner self, destroying all of my self esteem.

I stare into the mirror. My eyes are hollow and empty as a deep depression overtakes me.

I shower and cry silently to myself as the water burns through my bloody wounds.

On the third day, the wounds healed enough for me to go back to work. I slowly ready myself for work and leave.

I drive into the parking lot of the office, coercing my body to move.

I walk into the office, my body weakened and defeated from the physical and emotional pain it had endured just days earlier. I slowly walk up the stairs to my office, Andrew runs behind me.

"Jenna." He calls to me pleasantly. I turn to him, unable to hide my shattered expression. A look of concern immediately encompasses his face. He walks closer to me, placing his hands gently on my shoulders. He stares directly in my eyes

"Why are you so sad?" he asks me worriedly. He rubs my arms gently. His show of affection and concern touch me.

"Just a bad morning." I tell him with a slight smile. Kathleen walks over to us, and I pull away from Andrew, looking down.

"Are you feeling better Jenna?" Kathleen asks me sweetly. I nod my head, still looking down at the ground.

"I should really get to work, I've been out for a few days… I need to catch up." I tell them. They both nod, and I walk to my office.

"What's wrong with her?" Andrew asks Kathleen with wonder.

"She's married to Ben Kramer, that's what's wrong." Kathleen responds, shaking her head. She pats Andrews shoulder then walks away.

I sit at my desk, grieving over the latest beating I had received from Ben. My memory drifts back in to time. Back to the first time Ben ever put his hands on me.

It was shortly after we had been married. We were at a benefit for muscular dystrophy, and I had drunk quite a bit. I was only 18 years old at the time, so I handled myself much differently than I would now. I was laughing and flirting with a man when Ben walked up. I could tell by his expression he was very angry. He gripped my wrist tightly and forcibly pulled me out of the function to the limo. I, of course, not knowing what ensued deep within his sadistic mind, was so mad about his aggressive way of removing me from the function, that I made the mistake of sticking up for myself.

"Don't put your hands on me!" I yell as I pull my hands from him. I scoot over in the limo. Ben slams the door and turns to me. His eyes blazing as he moves closer to me. Without warning, he raises his hand and slaps me with vengeance across the face. I naturally defend myself and slap him back. Another regretful mistake I made. My slap only deepened his already vicious temperament. With a closed fist he hits me continuously, until I can no longer fight him back. I can feel my eyes swell, and taste the salty taste of blood as it runs down my nose and mouth. Ben takes his handkerchief out, and pats the blood from my face. Tears fill my eyes.

"Look what you made me do!" He says to me with disgust. His lack of affection and emotion for what he had done astounded me; I exhaled as I look down at the ground.

For days, I stayed locked up in the house, hiding Ben's secret. He left town, leaving me to wallow in my emotional struggle with all that had happened. I longed for him the longer he was away.

As the bruises and cuts from my face disappear, he returns. We never spoke of it, but I knew from that day forward that my life was always going to be this way.

The first year I spent with Ben was not learning his bad habits, like leaving the toothbrush in the sink, or clothes on the floor. It was learning Ben's unsaid rules and pet peeves, like wearing blue jeans, or wearing my hair down.

Ben's demented mind and psychotic ways led to many long nights in agony and pain. His beatings were light at first, but as I continued to break the rules his anger quickened and his beatings became more vicious.

To conceal the beatings from others, Ben only used his gold-buckle, dark brown leather belt, and was sure to only hit me in places that were covered by clothing.

I shake my head, staring down at my desk as the memory leaves me.

I worked till the afternoon, catching up on backed up paperwork in my office. I print out more reports for the attorney's and stroll down to the conference room. I walk to the table and organize the reports I had printed out for them. I reach across the table for a report, Andrew moves behind me as I move backwards. I can feel his breath on my neck.

"I thought you might need some help." he whispers to me. I look over my shoulder.

"I got it… thanks." I respond, smiling at him. I stare at the clock and it is lunch time.

"I'm going to lunch, I will print more reports when I get back." I say aloud. I walk out of the conference room and to the front door. Andrew follows me.

"Where are you going?" he asks me as I place my hand on the doorknob.

"I normally go to the cliff at lunch. It's by my house." I tell him.

"I could use some fresh air. Do you mind if I accompany you?" he asks. I shrug my shoulders. I walk out to the parking lot and Andrew follows, we decide that I will drive. I squeal out of the parking lot, and cut a car off instantly. Andrew places his hands firmly on the dashboard.

"I think I should have driven!" He says frantically. I laugh at him. I drive at top speed till we reach the cliff. I shut the car off and step out. Andrew opens his door and steps out, smiling.

"Wow. This is amazing!" He says as he gazes around at the trees and open land. I nod my head. I walk to the edge of the cliff and sit down, he follows suit, sitting next to me. The cliff has an open view of the lake and sandy beach below it.

The lake lives and wanders free, happy to flow gracefully with the wind. A serene piece of heaven, it mystifies me with its silent beauty.

I close my eyes, inhaling the fresh air, taking in the loving touch of nature. The light breeze caresses my face, I smile as I exhale. I take out my iPod and play my favorite mix of sad piano songs. The first song is "Journey"; sad, but so amazing.

"This is a beautiful view." He says to me.

"I know. I love it here." I tell him.

"Do you come here a lot?" he asks me.

"Any chance I can get. It's a place I can relax, and forget about everything. The closest place to heaven I know… Close your eyes and listen to lake, it sounds likes it's singing to you." I say to him quietly. He closes his eyes for a moment, and then opens them, smiling at me.

"I can hear it." He says with excitement.

"It's beautiful, isn't it?" He stares at me.

"It sure is." I change the music on my iPod and play "It's all on you." I had found the song accidently when I was surfing through YouTube and absolutely loved it. Andrew turns to me, smiling.

"This song is amazing, who sings it?" he asks me.

"I don't know, I found it by accident when I was surfing the Internet." He nods his head.

"What kind of music do you like?"

"Everything, as long as it is good."

I sit silently, staring out at the lake. I lift my knees and wrap my arms around them, not knowing I was exposing my lower back and the fading belt marks. Andrew notices them, he takes his fingers and gently touches them. I stand up immediately, pulling my shirt down.

"What happened?" he asks worriedly as he stands facing me.

"Nothing." I tell him quickly. I throw my iPod quickly into my purse, then throw my purse over my shoulder, and quickly stroll towards the parking lot, Andrew follows.

"Did I do something to offend you?" he asks me as we walk to my car.

"No. I just really have to get back, I missed a few days and I'm behind on my work." I tell him. We step into the car and I drive away.

"Jenna, what are those marks on your back?" he asks me with interest.

"I fell."

"They don't look like marks you would get from falling."

"Andrew, please. I really don't want to talk about it." I pull into the office parking lot, and shut off the car. I remove the keys from the ignition and place my hand on the door. Andrew places his hand gently on mine, stopping me. I turn to him.

"If you ever need to talk, I'm a good listener." He says sweetly. I smile at him.

"Thank you." I respond. We walk back into the office, Andrew walks to the conference room, and I walk upstairs.

I print more reports and walk back downstairs to the conference room.

"Jenna." I turn to the voice, and Ben is standing by the conference door. I immediately walk over to him. He places his hand in mine and walks me into the kitchen.

Ben and I sit down at the kitchen table. He places his hands in mine.

"I have to go to New Hampshire for a few days. I talked to Christie, and she said you could stay with her." He says to me. This brings a smile to my face. I loved spending time with Christie and Manny.

"Why are you going so long?" I ask him.

"We are going before the House with a proposal, and the Senator there is being stubborn, so I'm attempting to persuade her to come my way." He explains with a chuckle. I stare into his eyes and see it, that all too familiar smile that he gets when he's smitten with a new woman. I remember when that smile encompassed his face when he would look at me. I look down sadly. Ben places his index under my chin, lifting my eyes to his.

"Jenna, it's just business." He says softly. Tears fill my eyes.

"This is the same woman I saw you on television with?" I ask him tearfully. He smiles, wiping my tears.

"Jenna. Please don't get upset. She is just a co-worker. I promise nothing is going on between us." I nod my head, but I didn't believe him for one minute.

"Hey, I got you something." He says happily. He reaches into his pocket and takes out a black velvet jewelry box. He opens it, and inside is a ruby diamond necklace, with a matching bracelet and earrings, more confirmation that he was definitely having an affair with this woman. Whenever Ben started a new affair I received jewelry, I called it his guilt gift. I look up at him, and force a smile.

"It's beautiful." I tell him. I close the box and set it down on the table. He embraces me and nuzzles his face in my hair.

"I'll miss you." He says in a whisper.

"I'll miss you too." He pulls away and smiles at me.

"I really wish Rocco could go with you to your sisters. I am going to be so worried." He says to me, distraught. Manny despised Ben's overprotective nature and Rocco was never allowed at their house with me.

"I will be fine. Manny won't let anything happen to me." I tell him.

"I know." He responds softly. Although Ben despised Manny, and Manny despised Ben, Ben knew that Manny would take care of me and keep me safe.

Ben stands up, extending his hand to me. I take it and he walks to the front door. He wraps his arms around my waist and pulls me close, then places his lips gently on mine, kissing me passionately. After he finishes, he places his forehead to mine.

"I love you Jenna." He says quietly.

"I love you too." I respond to him. He kisses me quickly, and then turns, placing his hand on the doorknob.

"I'll call you when I get in." he tells me. I nod my head.

"Bye."

"Bye darling." He opens the door and leaves.

After Ben leaves, I walk back to the kitchen and retrieve the jewelry box. I open it up and stare at the contents. Andrew walks into the kitchen and over to me.

"What do you have there?" he asks with wonder. I hand it to him. He smiles as he stares at it.

"Ben bought it for me."

"It's very nice; your husband is very good to you." I nod my head. He hands me the jewelry box and I stare down at it. I must have frowned because Andrew walks closer to me. I look up at him.

"What's wrong, you don't like it?" he asks me, attempting to read my eyes. I shake my head.

"Of course I like it, it's very beautiful." I tell him. I can feel tears fill my eyes. I abruptly walk out of the kitchen, Andrew follows me. He places his hand on my arm, stopping me. I turn to him and tears fall down my face.

"What's wrong?" he asks me. His words only trigger more tears, crippling my already fragmented heart. He places his arm around me and walks me outside. I sit down on the porch, placing my face in my hands, sobbing. He sits next to me, draping his arm around me, attempting to comfort me. I attempt to regain my composure, wiping the tears from my face, I look up at him.

"I'm sorry." I tell him, sniffling. He smiles at me.

"No need to be sorry. I am just wondering what would make such a beautiful woman so sad." He says to me worriedly.

"It's personal." I tell him.

"I'm a good listener Jenna, you can trust me." I stare into his eyes, and could tell he was telling the truth.

"It's not the gift that makes me upset, it's the reason for the gift." I tell him. He nods.

"I'm listening."

"You know that woman, Senator Barker, we saw on the news with Ben?" I ask him.

"Yes."

"Ben is having an affair with her." I tell him disconcerted.

"How do you know?" he asks confused. I stare out.

"I know. It happens all the time. He goes away for a day, and then it turns into a couple of days. He buys me jewelry… It's all the same routine… I just know." I explain to him.

"This has happened before?" he asks me astounded.

"Yes. Many times."

"Why do you put up with it?" Andrew asks me, shaking his head.

"I love him so much, Andrew." I tell him tearfully.

"Jenna, he doesn't deserve your love if he treats you like this."

"Why, am I not enough for him? What's wrong with me?" I say, devastated. He embraces me.

"There is nothing wrong with you, it's not you, it's him."

The front door opens, Andrew and I pull away from each other, standing. Kathleen walks outside.

"What's going on here?" she asks with a smile.

"We were just talking, taking a break." Andrew responds. She nods her head.

"Ok. Well break is over, get back to work." Kathleen says to us. We both nod and walk inside.

I throw myself into my work, as I finish my last report and stare at the clock, and it reads 5:30. I shut my computer down and grasp my purse and rush out the door.

I stop at the liquor store, purchase a fifth of Tequila, and drive to the cliff.

The sun going down casts an orange glow across the lake. The water streams slowly in rhythm with the leaves of the trees. I breathe in the exhilarating, fresh air, and it brings an instant peace to me. I begin to feel inebriated as I chug down the bottle of Tequila, the more I drank, the more I desperately wanted freedom from the anguish that pierced so deeply in my heart. I dump my purse out, in need of my cell. I pick it up and call Andrew. He answers on the first ring.

"Andrew Carington?" he answers.

"Mr. Carington, I believe I want a divorce." I tell him.

"Mrs. Kramer, I am not married to you." He responds with a chuckle.

"I meant Ben, I want to divorce Ben!" I tell him tearfully. There is silence as I sob with grief.

"Jenna, where are you?" he whispers with concern.

"The cliff by my house." I answer.

"Where is your husband?" he asks with concern.

"I don't know." I respond sadly. I clear my throat, and regain my composure.

"Mr. Carington, are you going to help me get a divorce or not?" I yell madly. My cell goes dead. I stare down at it, and realize I had forgotten to charge it this morning. I exhale, and lay back on the grass, staring up at the clear beautiful sky.

A clinking sound awakens me and I open my eyes, staring up at the ceiling. I watch, as the ceiling fan rotates in sync with the sound. I close my eyes, shaking my head. I open my eyes again and gaze around the room, it's unfamiliar.

A dark cherry wood dresser sits in the corner, stacks of clothes piled on top of it. A black leather chair sits in the opposite corner, with another stack of clothes. There are clothes in small piles on the floor everywhere. I lay back down, curling to the pillow.

"Good morning." a voice says to me. It startles me, and with quick reflex, I pull the blankets up. I turn to my side and Andrew is lying next to me. I stare at him confused. I lift the covers looking underneath. Be it my luck, I am stark naked. I turn to Andrew.

"Did we?" I ask him with devastation.

"Of course we did." he responds with a smile.

"Oh, this is so bad!" I tell him nervously.

"Actually, it was pretty good." he says with sarcasm. His sarcastic tone fills me with irritation.

"I can't believe you took advantage of me when I was drunk." I say to him with irritation.

"Me? It was not I who took advantage of you. It was you, who took advantage of me, you are quite convincing when you are only wearing this." He holds up the corset, grinning.

His grin infuriates me. I stand, wrapping the blanket around me, pulling it off of him, exposing his naked body. I stare at his perfect body. His muscular chest arouses me. The V-shaped line that encompasses his lower abdomen sends my hormones into overdrive. He smiles as he watches me gaze at his body.

"You like what you see?" he asks with a smirk. I turn away from him.

"You are so unbelievably arrogant!" I say with irritation. He stands, sliding his boxers on.

He walks behind me, sliding his hands softly up and down my arms. Goosebumps instantly appear on my arms as his touch sends a tingling sensation through my body. He smiles and wraps his arms around my waist, pulling me close to him.

"I turn you on." he whispers in my ear.

The warmth of his breath encompasses my whole body. He kisses my neck softly. I close my eyes, embracing his touch. He places his lips to mine. I clutch his back, tightly inviting his kiss. The blanket falls and he scoops me into his arms, carrying me back to the bed, never letting his lips leave mine. He lies me down gently, sliding on top of me.

A fire releases through his lips, igniting every nerve in my body as he kisses me. I clutch his back tightly, needing to feel his body close to mine. He kisses my neck softly. I tilt my head allowing him access. He slides his lips down my neck and I am so aroused I feel as if I will completely combust, as every kiss, every touch brings me closer to the edge. He moves down my body to my breast, twirling his tongue around my nipple, suckling it softly. I moan loudly as he kisses my stomach, moving still down my body. He kisses my thighs and my body starts to shiver, he places his hands under my thighs, lifting them gently, and moving between my legs. The soft twirl of his tongue inside me is more than my body can handle, and within seconds I find my release.

"Oh!" I moan, closing my eyes as my body convulses with pleasure. My breathing is so rapid I have to open my mouth to suck in air. I don't even notice Andrew is no longer in the bed. I only notice when he moves on top of me. The fresh, minty smell of his breath is tantalizing, as he places his lips to mine.

I engulf him completely. He takes his hand, and gently spreads my knees apart, then enters inside of me.

The want for him was so deep, my mind wandered into a world of complete ecstasy. Every movement of his body syncs instantly with mine. I start to build up as he slowly moves inside of me. He kisses me, panting as he is building up, too. I wrap my legs around him, wanting him deeper inside of me. When I feel as if it couldn't feel any better, he begins to move faster and it happens. I come undone instantly, finding my release once again. Andrew follows soon after. I am paralyzed, I can't move. My body still convulses as he is still inside of me.

As he regains his strength he pulls out of me, lying to my side. He wraps his arms around me tightly, facing me.

"You're trembling." he says softly. I am breathless and unable to speak, so I just nod.

I lay on the bed, staring up at the ceiling, with Andrew's arms wrapped around me. He moves his hand tenderly up and down my arm.

"Is this an affair?" I ask him. He lifts his head, using his hand to support it.

"Do you want it to be an affair?" he asks me. I shrug my shoulders.

"I don't know… I just know this isn't right." I tell him. He exhales.

"Because you're married?" he asks me. I nod my head distraught.

"Yes."

"This is what you call a one night stand. You are really quite naïve, aren't you?" he asks with an irritating laugh.

"What do you mean by that?" I respond, annoyed. He chuckles at my reaction. He places his hand, gently rubbing my frown lines.

"You should be careful, your forehead will stay like that." he says with sarcasm. I stand, pulling the blankets off of him yet again. He chuckles loudly.

"It amazes me how dark your hazel eyes become when you are angry. You are quick tempered." he says, amused.

"I'm happy that I amuse you, Mr. Carington." I snap angrily. Shaking his head, he crawls across the bed and reaches to me, pulling me back on the bed. He embraces me tightly.

"Turn that frown upside down baby." he says cutely. I smile at him. "That's better." he responds to me. He places his lips to mine kissing me softly. Remembering his words from earlier I pull away from him.

"One night stands are supposed to be one time right?" I ask him. He chuckles at my comment.

"Touché, Mrs. Kramer."

"So we have already broken the rules." I attempt to stand up but he wraps his arms around me, pulling me back to him.

"I don't believe in rules." He smirks.

"Your playtime is over Mr. Carington." I say with a quiet grin. I attempt to pull away from him, but he tightens his embrace on me.

"Oh no, playtime has just started." He responds smiling.

After we make love once again, I dress and Andrew drives me to the cliff, dropping me off at my car.

Andrew parks and steps out, opening my door. I step out of the car.

"I had a really good time." I grimace at my comment. "Sorry, I…uh. Oh boy." I say at a loss of words.

"It's okay Jenna." he giggles.

"I'll see you later." I tell him. I walk to my car and drive to Christies.

I decided to call into work. I was tired from my night with Andrew. I lie on the bed, wanting a quick nap. My cell buzzes as I close my eyes, I pick it up.

"Where are you?" Andrew texts.

"I took the day off." I text back.

"Oh I see. Did I wear you out Mrs. Kramer?"

"No. Actually it was quite boring."

"Boring!!!!!!!!!!"

"Just playing."

"Playing? I would love to play with you again…"

"Oh yeah?"

"Yeah. Playtime is very pleasurable with you Mrs. Kramer."

"Playtime and Mrs. Kramer, sounds like you're getting it on with your teacher. It's very creepy."

"I just spit hot coffee all over your reports after reading that comment."

"You better have not! I worked hard on those reports."

"I guess you will have to work late re-printing tomorrow, don't worry, I'll stay with you."

"I bet you would. I have to nap now, you have fun at work!"

"Sweet dreams, dream of me." I smile as I place my cell in purse. I curl up to the pillow and drift off to sleep.

Christie comes home at about 7:00, waking me up.

"Where were you last night?" she asks me.

"I went home." I lie.

"Oh… it's Friday night, you want to go to the pub?" she asks me with a smile.

"Yeah!"

"Well, get ready then."

I shower quickly and walk into the bedroom, clad only in a towel. I gaze through the closet for something to wear. I pick out a black skirt and a black strapless top. I pair it off with a pair of black heeled boots. Ben always made me wear my hair up, because he said I needed to look like a lady at all times, and not have my hair flowing about in my face. I dry my hair, and then put big curls in it; I lightly brush it so it lay perfectly to the middle of my back. I put my makeup on extra thick, and finish with red lipstick. I pick out silver, dangling earrings, with a matching necklace, and a lot of bracelets. I walk out to the living room and Christie stands, smiling.

"Now that's my sister!" She says proudly. I grab a black bolero jacket and put it on.

It was Friday night, so I was not surprised that the Pub parking lot was packed. Christie parks near the back and we step out of the car and walk through the parking lot.

We pass a crowd of three men as we walk towards the back door. They surround us smiling. A muscular man with blonde hair and dark eyes walks up to Christie and me.

"Hello ladies." He says with a smile. Christie rolls her eyes and walks closer to him.

"Excuse us." She says to him madly. He laughs at her.

"Why are you in such a rush?" he asks her.

"Can you please move out of my way?" Christie says as she attempts to push past him. He places his hands on her arms, stopping her, and smiles.

"Release her, now." A voice says behind us. I turn, and Andrew Carington walks up with Eric and Matt. He walks over to the man, and grabs Christie from him.

"Back off!" Andrew yells angrily. The man laughs, then gestures to his friends and they leave.

"Are you okay?" Andrew asks Christie with concern.

"Yeah. Thanks. Who are you?" she asks him. I walk up to her.

"He is Andrew Carington, our attorney." I explain to her. She nods to me.

"What is your name?" Andrew asks her.

"Christie, I am Jenna's sister."

"It's nice to meet you, Christie." Andrew says politely.

"I need a drink." She says as she places her arm in mine, and we walk in.

We all sit near the dance floor. I gaze at Andrew and exhale softly. He is dressed in a button up black shirt and blue jeans with black high tops. He stands next to me, taking a lock of my dark brown hair in his hands.

"I didn't know your hair was so long. I like it down." He says to me. I smile at him.

"Thank you." I respond softly. The waitress walks over to us.

"What can I get you folks?" she asks us. Andrew turns to me.

"What would you like, Jenna?" he asks me.

"A Margarita." I tell him. He turns to Christie.

"Christie?" he asks her.

"I'll take a margarita, too." She tells him. Andrew nods. He orders and the waitress walks away.

The place is swarming with people, and I become so hot that I remove my jacket. I sit down at the table and Andrew sits next to me. Christie and Eric engage in a conversation. Andrew slides his hand gently across my shoulder. I turn to him.

"You look so different." Andrew says to me.

"What do you mean?" I ask him.

"You dress too conservative, like a Senator's wife, you look more your age tonight." He tells me.

"I don't know whether to be offended or thankful for that comment."

"It's a compliment. I told you before you are way too young to be a Senator's wife." Not wanting to pursue that conversation again. I smile at him.

"Thank you, Andrew. What brings you to the Pub?"

"Eric comes here a lot. I tagged along this time." Andrew answers. I nod my head.

A small petite woman with dark eyes and hair approaches our table; she smiles at Andrew as she walks up.

"Hi Andrew." She says smiling.

"Hi Jordan." He responds blandly.

"I didn't know you came here." She continues.

"I don't." he responds, blowing her off. She stands behind Andrew, and he completely ignores her.

"I guess I'll see you around." She says sadly. She turns, still staring at Andrew and slowly walks away. I lean towards him.

"Who was that?" I ask him.

"Just some girl, I used to see her once in awhile." He responds.

"Oh. Are you always that rude to girls you used to see once in a while?" I ask him with sarcasm.

"I have to be, I don't want to lead her on. If I'm nice to her, she will hang around me all night long, and I don't want that." He explains.

"The polite thing to say would be, 'I am busy can I talk to you later?'"

"Jenna, women are complicated. If you're nice to them, they want more, if you ignore them, they want more. It doesn't matter what I do, they always seem to want more from me." He continues. His arrogant nature appalls me once again.

"You are awfully sure of yourself, Mr. Carington."

"I'm just stating a fact." I exhale, rolling my eyes at him.

Andrew and I talk and drink all night long. Christie and I do shots of Tequila throughout the night; it is not long until we are both completely hammered. Christie calls Manny to pick her up as she becomes too inebriated to drive. I decide to stay at the request of Andrew. He makes a promise to Christie he will make sure I get home safely. I stand and stumble. Andrew places his arm around me.

"I believe you have had just a little too much to drink, Jenna." Andrew says with a smirk.

"You are so cute, do you know that?" I respond as I touch his face softly. He chuckles. A slow song begins to play.

"Dance with me." I say, slurring, I don't wait for an answer; I take his hand and drag him out to the floor. I trip as we reach the dance floor, and he catches me. I stare into his eyes. It's like a light surrounds him, and his blue eyes glisten at me.

"You are so beautiful." I say to him as I place my hand gently on his cheek.

I don't remember what happened next. All I remember is waking up in the morning to my pounding head. I sit up, rubbing my head. I stare around the room and realize I am again at Andrew's. I turn to the side of me, and see him sleeping next to me. I start to panic. I look under the covers and see that I am completely naked, again.

"Oh no, not again!" I say, disappointed in myself. Andrew chuckles as he sits up in the bed.

"We really have to stop meeting like this." He says to me, still chuckling.

"How the hell did I end up here, again?" I ask him, confused.

"You don't remember?" he asks me.

"No."

"We were at the pub, you were drinking… One thing led to another, and now we're here." He explains to me.

"I really need to stop drinking."

"I assure you it is not the alcohol that attracts you to me. Just admit to yourself you find me irresistible." Andrew states, with a cocky grin.

"How many times a day do you kiss the mirror?" I respond with disgust.

"Every time." he retorts. I hear my cell ring and look for it. The door opens, and Eric walks in. Andrew pulls the covers up and over me.

"Can't you knock?" Andrew yells angrily.

"Sorry. I heard Jenna's phone ringing so I brought her purse in here." He says, holding my purse up. Andrew gestures to him and Eric walks over to the bed handing it to him.

"Thanks." He says softly. Eric nods his head and then smiles as he stares at me. "Leave, Eric!" Andrew tells him madly. Eric turns and walks out of the room, closing the door.

Andrew hands my purse to me, and I rummage through it in search of my cell. I lift my wallet and find my cell underneath. I pull it out and look at my missed calls. I look up at Andrew nervously.

"It's Ben." I tell him.

I wrap the blankets around me and stand, exposing yet again Andrew's naked body. I call Ben, he answers on the first ring.

"Hi darling." Ben says happily.

"Hi." I respond to him.

"You sound sleepy. I couldn't get a hold of you so I called Christie. She told me you were still asleep. I'm sorry darling, for leaving you for so many days alone. I am going to try very hard to lessen my travel schedule." I feel Andrews arms wrap around me as he kisses my neck softly. I lightly exhale.

"It's okay." I respond immediately.

Andrew lightly pulls the blanket from around me, dropping it to the ground. He runs his hands up and down my body gently as he kisses my shoulders. I close my eyes as his touch sends a deep sensation through my body.

"I should be home this evening. I'm leaving from New Hampshire right now." Ben continues.

"Ok." I tell him breathlessly. Andrew turns me to face him. He nuzzles his face in my hair, nibbling on my ear.

"I love you. I will see you soon."

"I love you too. Bye." I hang the cell up and let it fall to the ground. I wrap my arms around Andrew, placing my lips to his.

After we make love, I search the bedroom for my clothes and find only my corset, panties, and thigh highs. I walk into the bathroom and use Andrew's toothbrush, then place the corset on.

As I am attaching the thigh highs, Andrew walks in. I move to the side and he brushes his teeth. I attach the last thigh high and he walks over to me.

Without warning, he lifts me up, placing me on the bathroom counter, and then moves so he is standing in between my legs. He stares at me for a moment, then tilts his head, kissing me. His kisses burn through me, I am aroused instantly. I wrap my legs around him, pulling him closer to me.

"Hey. Here's Jenna's shirt and skirt." Eric says as he walks into the bathroom. I release my legs instantly and Andrew stands so he his blocking me from Eric.

"Can you please knock?" Andrew says to him madly.

"I did knock but you didn't answer." Eric responds defensively. He walks over to Andrew, handing my dress to him. He stares at me, smiling.

"Eric, go." Andrew states firmly. Eric nods and leaves. Andrew smiles as he hands me my shirt and skirt. I slide my shirt on and stand as I step into my skirt. I walk to the bedroom and Andrew rushes up behind me, scooping me in his arms laying me on the bed. He smiles as he moves on top of me.

"What are you doing?"

"I'm going to make love to you again."

"Andrew I don't think"—Andrew interrupts me, placing his finger across my lips.

"Don't think." He responds as he places his lips to mine, kissing me softly.

Chapter III

Andrew's bathroom definitely screamed, "Bachelor". Not a hand towel in the place as I attempt to wash up. I walk near the shower and find a bath towel. I dry my hands and face, then walk out to the bedroom. Andrew is fully dressed and sliding his shoes on.

"I'm going to take you to your sisters." he says politely. I nod my head. We walk out of the bedroom and to the front door.

I sit silently as we drive to Christies. Andrew parks. He steps out of the car, walking over to my side, opening the door. I step out of the car.

"I'll see you later." I tell him. I turn and walk towards the door.

"Jenna." Andrew says to me. I stop and turn and he walks over so he is standing in front of me.

He bends his head slightly, kissing me. I clutch his back as he embraces me tightly. When we are finished I exhale with my eyes closed.

"I am not working at the office today. So I will see you tomorrow."

"Ok." He smiles and walks back to his car. I walk into Christies and she has already left for work, I felt an instant relief. I definitely did not feel like explaining my whereabouts to her.

I shower and quickly, get ready, and head off to the office.

I sit at my desk, tapping my pen, thinking of Andrew. What we were doing was wrong, but my want for him was so deep and unexplainable. The day dragged, and when 5:30 came, I was happy to leave.

As I walk down the office stairs my cell buzzes. I sit down on the last step and retrieve it from my purse. I smile as it's a text from Andrew.

"Hello." He text.

"Hi."

"Are you leaving work yet?"

"I was just leaving when you texted me."

"I see. Are you going home?"

"Yes."

"Can you come out and play?"

"You are becoming quite spoiled."

"Not spoiled, just enjoy being with you."

"I enjoy being with you also. But I can't tonight, I have to go home."

"I really am disappointed. I was hoping I could see you tonight."

"We have other nights."

"I suppose, I guess I'll see you tomorrow then."

"Ok, see you tomorrow." I slide my cell into my purse and leave.

I sit in my car, thinking of Andrew for a moment then slide out and walk in to the house.

The house is lit only by candles as I walk in. I place my purse down on the counter. Ben walks into the kitchen, smiling.

"Hi darling." He says to me, kissing me on the cheek.

"What is all of this?" I ask him. He places his arms around my waist.

"It's for you… I have drawn a bath for you." He says as he places his hand in mine, and we walk through the bedroom to the bathroom.

Ben undresses me, and I step into the bath. He walks over; grasping a sponge in his hand, then washes my back. He kisses my neck softly and I close my eyes, embracing his touch. He stands, undressing, then slides into the bath behind me, wrapping his arms around me.

"I missed you so much, Jenna." He says as he places tender kisses across my back. I smile at him. He lets his arms roam across my body, and I can feel he is aroused.

He places his hands on my hips, turning me to face him.

"Get on top." He says softly. I stand up and straddle him, slowly sliding down on him.

"Oh yeah." He says as I slowly move up and down on him.

I grimace as the act of making love to Ben all of a sudden disgusts me. He grasps my breasts in his hands, pulling hard on my nipples.

"Come on Jenna, move faster." He says to me with a scorned look. I grasp the sides of the tub for support and move up and down faster on him. He places his hands on my hips and slams me down on him.

"Ow!" I scream as he rips inside of me. My scream of pain only arouses him even more, and he slams me on him over and over.

He screams as he finds his release. I attempt to move from atop of him, but he stops me.

"Don't move yet." He snaps at me. I sit still till Ben is ready. He gently places his hands on my hips, lifting me as he pulls out of me.

He steps out of the bath tub and walks into the bedroom. The water burns as I sit down in it, instantly the water is a pinkish color. I wrap a towel around me and walk to the bedroom. Ben is already in bed; I slide in and cuddle close to him. I kiss his neck lightly.

"Jenna, I'm exhausted." He states. I lie back down on my pillow, staring at the back of his head.

Unable to sleep, I decide to take a walk to the cliff. The night was starting to encompass the sky, and I could see the red glare of the sun going down. I inhale the fresh breeze of the wind, closing my eyes. I can hear the hum of the leaves on the trees as they sing in harmony with the wind. I stretch out across the grass, staring up at the stars.

I wake in the morning, desolate. I felt detached from my own heart, as confusion fills my mind. The love I had felt so deep for Ben, was slowly turning only into a memory. The intimacy and desire for him had simply disappeared. The thought of making love to him was now just a dreaded obligation. I turn to Ben's side, and a note is lying on his pillow.

"*Darling,*

I had a call from the Senator in Maine. He could only meet today, so I will be out of town for a few days. I need another favor, please call me when you wake.

Love you,

Ben."

I grasp my cell and call Ben.

"Hello." I say quietly.

"Hi darling." Ben responds.

"Hi."

"I left some papers on the nightstand in the bedroom. It is very imperative that you take them to the attorneys for me today." He says to me.

"Ok."

"I love you." I sit silently, as I can't even choke out the words.

"Jenna?" I clear my throat.

"I love you too." I say, grimacing. I hang up my cell.

I ready myself for my trip to the attorneys. I grasp my purse and the papers from the nightstand, and walk out to the limo with Rocco in tow.

I sit in the waiting area for Andrew. He walks up to me.

"Jenna." He says with a smile.

"Andrew." I respond. He instantly notices my distant demeanor and kneels in front of me.

"What's wrong?" he asks me quietly.

"Nothing. I'm just tired, that's all." He stands up.

"If you are ready, we can go to my office." He says to me. I stand up and follow him to his office. Rocco stays behind in the waiting room.

We reach Andrews office and he walks over to the leather couch, sitting down. I sit down on the couch across from him. I hand him the papers, he gazes over them as I stare down at the ground. He tilts his eyes up at me.

"Are you sure you're okay?" he asks me. I nod my head. He places the papers on the table and sits back on the couch, staring at me. I look up at him.

"What is it?" I ask him as he continues to stare at me. He sits forward.

"Tell me what's wrong?" he asks with persistency.

"Nothing. Are we finished? Can I go?" I ask him impatiently.

"No. Not until you tell me what's wrong with you?" he asks again. I stand up.

"Andrew I assure you I am quite fine. I am just a little tired, that's all. If we are finished I would really like to go." I tell him. He nods his head.

I walk towards the door and he follows. I reach for the doorknob, and he places his hand on mine, stopping me. He moves so he is standing behind me so close I can hear his heart beat. He nuzzles his face in my hair.

"Where are you going?" he whispers seductively in my ear.

"I have to go home." I answer nervously. He turns me so I'm facing him. He stares into my eyes. I close my eyes.

"Please Andrew, I need to leave." I tell him with desperation.

"Why?" He kisses my neck softly. I exhale.

"I can't."

"You can't what." He says as he unbuttons my shirt. He places his hands on my shoulder, pushing my shirt off, it falls to the ground. He kisses my shoulder gently.

"Please stop." I say with a light moan.

"You don't want me to stop." He slowly unzips my skirt, and it falls to the ground. He gazes at me as I am only clad in a tan camisole and matching panties. He locks the door, and then with one swift move, he scoops me into his arms. He places his lips to mine as he carries me to the leather couch. He lies me down then undresses down to his boxers.

A knock on his office door interrupts us. I stand up and rush over to the door, grasping my clothes. I run into the bathroom, closing the door. Andrew dresses quickly and walks to the door, opening it.

"Why is your door locked?" A man asks him. I walk out of the bathroom fully clothed and I see an older version of Andrew standing next to him. He smiles at me.

"Father, this is Jenna Kramer. Senator Kramer's wife… Jenna this is my father, William." Andrew introduces. William smiles at me as he walks up to me, shaking my hand.

"It's a pleasure to finally meet you, Jenna. Ben talks about you all the time." William says to me.

"It's nice to meet you too, Mr. Carington." I respond politely.

"William. Please call me William."

"William."

"So what brings you to our office?" William asks me.

"Ben asked me to drop off some paperwork." I tell him.

"I see. Well, sorry for the interruption." William says to us. He walks towards the door. "Son, can I talk to you outside for a moment."

"Of course." Andrew answers immediately

"Excuse me." Andrew says to me politely. I nod my head, and sit down on the couch. Andrew walks out to the hall with William, closing the door.

"What are you up to Andrew?" William asks him.

"Nothing, just meeting with Mrs. Kramer." Andrew answers. William takes his finger and wipes Andrew's lip. He holds it up, and lipstick is on his finger. Andrew squeezes his eyes closed quickly, and then looks down with embarrassment.

"She is a married woman. Her husband is very powerful, and not someone you want to mess with. Whatever it is you think you are doing, you stop it this instant!" William says, scolding him.

Andrew nods and William walks away. Andrew walks back into the office; he sits on the couch across from me, and snatches the papers from the table. I sit quietly, looking down.

"It looks like everything is here." Andrew says to me. I look up at him.

"Thank you Andrew."I respond to him.

An uncomfortable silence encompasses the room as we both sit, staring down at the ground. I stand and walk towards the door. I grasp the doorknob.

"Jenna!" Andrew blurts out. I turn and he rushes up to me.

He kisses me with urgency; he picks me up and carries me into the bathroom, closing the door. He places me on the ground. We kiss, messy and hard, Andrew drops his pants and boxers, closes the lid of the toilet, and sits down. He place his hands on my hips, pulling me to him, he slides his hands up my skirt, pulling my panties off. I straddle him, and then slowly I sit, placing him inside of me.

"Oh." Andrew says as I slowly move up and down on him. He cups my breasts in his hand as I move faster and faster on top of him.

"Oh…oh." I scream as I find my release, Andrew follows quickly after. He rubs my back gently as I sit, breathless. I stand, and slide my panties on. Andrew slides his boxers and pants on. He gently pushes me against the wall, kissing me softly.

"I have to go." I say to him quietly. He nods, smiling at me. I exit the bathroom and walk out of the office. Rocco stands as I walk to the waiting room.

"Are you ready to go?" he asks me.

"Yes." I respond. We exit the building, and walk to the limo. I shower as soon as I get home. I walk into the bedroom and sit on the bed, clad only in a towel, refreshed from my visit with Andrew.

My cell buzzes. I pick it up, and it's a text from Andrew.

"You definitely put a permanent grin on my face today."

"I aim to please."

"Oh baby, that you sure do, pleasing me that is."

"Are you flirting with me, Andrew?"

"Always."

"I really have to go. I do have other things to do besides texting you."

"How about you come back to my office… and show me these other things?"

"You sure are greedy."

"That I am."

"I cannot today, maybe another day."

"You have my number, I am available to you anytime."

"I will keep that in mind. Have a pleasant afternoon."

"You too."

I sit around watching sitcoms for the rest of the night. As I become tired, I walk to the bedroom. I ready myself for bed and slide under the covers. I stare up at the ceiling as I think of Andrew. I curl to my pillow and drift off to sleep.

Ben slides into bed, cuddling close to me. I turn to the clock and it is 1:00 a.m. I close my eyes and fall back to sleep.

I wake in the morning and shower. I walk out to the bedroom and Ben is sliding his shoes on. He stands, kissing me.

"I will see you tonight." He says to me.

"Okay, Bye." I respond.

I finish getting ready and rush out to work. I drive into the parking lot and scurry inside.

Eric and Matt are already in the conference room when I arrive. I walk in and get right to work. Fifteen minutes later, Andrew walks in. I look up at him, and he winks at me as he approaches Eric and Matt.

"I need you and Matt to go to the Troy job. They have a few issues that are not being met by the attorney's I have sent there. I need you two to help them." Andrew explains to Eric.

"Ok. When do you want us to go?" Eric asks Andrew.

"Now. I'll stay here and work on this project." Andrew responds.

Eric nods and with Matt in tow leaves, closing the conference door. Andrew walks over to it, quietly locking it. He stares at me slowly, walking towards me. I turn to face him, smiling.

"What is on your mind?" I ask him, grinning. He places his arms around me, pulling me close.

"You. You are what's on my mind." He responds as slides his hand slowly down my arm.

"It's not playtime, Andrew. We are working." I tell him sternly. I tap his hand playfully, and pull away from him. I begin stacking the reports when he walks up behind me. He kisses my shoulder softly, as he runs his hands gently down my arms, arousing me instantly. He smirks as he feels the goose bumps encompass my arms.

"Your body is defying you. Its telling me it is definitely play time." He whispers in my ear. I turn to face him.

He takes me in his arms, kissing me with desperation. Our hands roam aimlessly across each other's body as we give in to our desire. Andrew moves me so I am pressed against the wall. He rips my panties to shreds as he removes them. I unbutton and unzip his pants, urgently pushing them down. He lifts me, and enters inside of me. I wrap my legs around him. It lasts minutes, until we both find our release. I stare at Andrew, breathless. I remove my legs from around him, standing, and slide my skirt down. He pulls his pants up, buttoning and zipping them. He bends down to the floor, picking up my torn panties, he smiles as he slides them into his pants pocket.

"I'm going to keep these." he says with a smile. I smile back. He places his hand on my cheek, kissing me softly.

"We need to work." I tell him. He chuckles, nodding. He walks over to the conference door and unlocks it.

Eric and Matt arrive back at the office around 12:30, and we all decide to break for lunch.

Andrew and I step into the back seat and we leave. As we are driving down the road, Andrew places his hand in mine. I turn, smiling at him.

The restaurant we decide on is busy. Unable to get a table, I walk up, and use Ben's name, and instantly they seat us. Andrew pulls out my chair, and I sit, he sits next to me. The waiter brings over menus, and I gaze across mine.

Andrew places his hand on my knee, under the table. I turn to him and smile. I continue to gaze across the menu and he slowly moves his hand under my dress, stroking my thigh. A fire begins to ignite as he moves his hand farther up my thigh.

"Jenna, thanks for getting us a table." Eric says to me.

"No problem." I respond to him.

My breath quickens as Andrew slides his hand between my legs. I turn to him nervously and he smiles. He moves his face closer to mine.

"What's wrong?" he asks in a whisper.

"Please stop." I respond to him in a panic.

"As you wish." He says as he withdraws his hand, smiling.

Lunch went by fast, and before I knew it we were driving back to the office.

We walk into the office, I turn to Andrew and a large grin is on his face.

"Why are you grinning?" I ask him confused.

"I'm always grinning when I'm around you." he responds cutely. I smile and walk into the kitchen. I open the fridge and take out a diet cola. Andrew follows behind me.

I take a sip of my diet cola and stare at a magazine sitting on the island. He walks behind me and wraps his arms around me. I pull away from him.

"You can't do that here." I say in a whisper. He wraps his arms around me tightly.

"I can do whatever I want to." He responds, smirking. He slides his hand up my thigh. I tap his hand lightly.

"Mr. Carington we are working, it is not play time." I tell him. He places both of his hands on my thighs and slowly runs them up my skirt.

"It's always play time when I'm with you." He whispers in my ear. He kisses my softly on the neck and I become aroused.

"Hey Andrew"—Eric says as he interrupts us. I pull away from Andrew. "Sorry, am I interrupting something?" Eric asks us.

"I will see you later." I say to Andrew nervously. I walk briskly up to my office.

I sit at my desk when my cell buzzes.

"Play time tonight?" he texts, I smile at his text.

"You are becoming awfully greedy."

"Not greedy, just needy." I laugh loudly. My office door opens and Andrew walks in, smiling. He sits on the edge of my desk. I chuckle, shaking my head.

"I am happy that I amuse you Jenna." He says with a smile.

"That you definitely do." I respond to him.

"So, what about tonight?" he asks me.

"I can't. I have this benefit I have to attend." I tell him.

"The Capatcha benefit?" he asks.

"Yes. How did you know?"

"I was invited; however, I would rather spend time with you." He slides his finger down my cleavage. I grasp his finger.

"Unfortunately, I have to go." I say as I release his finger. He stands and walks towards the door. He stops as he grasps the doorknob, turning to look at me.

"Well then, I guess I'll see you there." He smiles and leaves.

The Capatcha Country Club is the largest country club in Michigan. It was a members' only club, and the requirements for membership were money and power.

The limo pulls up to the front. Ben opens the door, extending his hand to me. I take it and he helps me out of the limo. We walk up to the front and immediately we are met by Christian Keyes, the organizer of the benefit.

"Ah. The Kramers!" Christian says with a smile. Ben shakes his hand. Christian turns around and waves his hand, and over walks Andrew. A smile encompasses my face, until I see his hand in the hand of a beautiful, thin, tall blonde. I gasp, barely able to breathe.

"Senator Kramer." Andrew says to him politely.

"Hello Andrew. Who is this lovely woman you are with Andrew?" Ben asks him.

"This is Kelly Keyes." he responds politely. It's apparent she is Christian Keyes daughter, as he walks over to her, kissing her on the cheek, and the fact they both had the same last name. I glare at Kelly.

"It's very nice to meet you, Kelly." Ben says nicely.

They make small talk then leave. Ben takes my hand, kissing it.

"I am going in the back; they have a card game going. Do you want to go home? Or stay?" he asks me.

"I will stay." I tell him. They often had illegal card games in the back rooms of these benefits, and, of course, Ben always participated in them. He kisses me quickly and leaves.

I stand, staring at Andrew and Kelly dancing slowly together, smiling at each other. A jealous rage fires deep within me. Eric walks up to me.

"Hi Jenna." He says sweetly. I place my hand in his.

"Dance with me." I tell him. I don't wait for an answer. I drag him out to the dance floor. Andrew stares at me and I turn my head. I pull Eric close to me. I smile as I look up at him, and gently play with his hair. He blushes at my touch.

"So Eric, what are your plans tonight?" I ask him.

"Just the benefit, that's all. Then home and sleep." He responds to me.

"I see." I can feel Andrew's glare on me. I pull Eric closer to me. He looks at me nervously.

"Mrs. Kramer, your husband." He says to me. I move my lips to his ear.

"Don't worry, my husband is in a card game. He won't be back for hours." I whisper seductively to Eric.

"Oh." Eric responds nervously. I pull away from Eric.

"I'm hot, do you want to go outside and get some air?" I ask Eric. He nods. We walk off the dance floor and walk towards the door, when Andrew runs up to us. He grasps my hand, pulling me backwards.

"Where are you going?" He asks me worriedly.

"Eric and I were just walking outside to get some air." I tell him, confused by his worried expression. Kelly walks up to us, she looks at Andrew strangely.

"Why did you leave me on the dance floor?" Kelly asks him madly.

"I'm sorry. I really need to talk to Jenna. I saw her walking towards the door and wanted to catch her before she left, it's about work." Andrew explains to Kelly quickly.

"What do you need to talk to me about?" I ask him with a raised eyebrow.

"It's private." He whispers. He turns to Kelly. "I will be right back." He tells her. She nods and he walks towards the bathrooms with me in tow.

He grasps my hand, and pulls me into a closet, closing the door.

"So what did you want to talk about?" I ask him with wonder.

"Do I not please you enough?" he asks me seductively. I swallow hard at his comment.

"What is this all about?" I ask him. He gently pins me against the wall with his body. I gasp as I can feel his erection against my leg. He gently slides his hand up my thigh. He nuzzles his face in my hair.

"I said, 'do I not please you enough'?" he whispers in my ear. His soft whisper sends chills up and down my spine.

"You please me enough." I murmur breathlessly.

He stares into my eyes as he lifts my dress and removes my panties. Then he unbuckles his pants and drops them. He places gentle kisses on my neck then enters inside of me.

"Andrew." I say as he moves faster inside of me.

"That's right baby, say my name." he responds panting.

My eyes roll back in my head as I find myself engulfed in him. I close my eyes, embracing all of him. He enters inside of me faster and faster. I clutch his back as I climb quickly.

"Oh… Andrew!" I respond loudly as I find my release.

"Oh… Jenna!" He says as he follows. He pulls out of me and I bend, sliding my panties on as he pulls his pants up. As he buckles his belt, he presses me against the wall again with his body.

"No more Eric." He whispers in my ear with seriousness. I nod my head.

He opens the door, peeking out, then leaves. I stand inside the closet, still trembling from my quick encounter with Andrew. I open the door and walk out of the closet. I walk out near the dance floor. Andrew is talking to Kelly, he looks over at me and smiles, I smile back.

Ben walks over to me.

"What happened?" I ask him.

"I lost again." He responds smirking. A petite brunette woman walks up to us. She immediately hugs Ben. I watch as Ben's hand slides down her behind as he embraces her tightly. I fill with rage instantly.

"Hillary Barker, this is my wife, Jenna." Ben introduces. She shakes my hand.

"It's very nice to meet you, Jenna." She says pleasantly. I glare at her. My glare surprises and embarrasses Ben.

"Jenna, Hillary is the senator of New Hampshire; she is who I visited when I was away." He tells me. The anger fills me even more as he admits to being with her. I succumb to the jealous rage that filled me instantly.

"Oh. Did you visit her in her bed? Or yours?" I say madly. Hillary gasps.

"Excuse me?" She says, appalled. Ben grasps my wrist tightly.

"I apologize, Hillary… Excuse me please." Ben says simply. With his hand tightly around my wrist, he walks away, instantly pulling me behind him. He stops near the front door.

"What the hell are you doing?" he says enraged.

"Me? Tell me what you were doing in New Hampshire with her." I retort. He pulls on my wrist tighter.

"My business matters do not concern you." He snaps.

"Especially when it comes to the women you sleep with… Why did you ever marry me?" I ask him sadly. Tears fill my eyes. He looks at me, devastated by my comment.

"Good evening Mr. and Mrs. Kramer." I look up and Andrew is standing in front of us. Ben releases my wrist, smiling at Andrew. I wipe the tears from my eyes.

"Andrew." Ben says shaking his hand.

"Senator." He responds. I continue to look down, distraught. Ben turns to me placing his index finger under my chin, lifting my eyes to his.

"Darling, I'm going to the bar, would you like anything?" he asks me.

"Red wine, please." I respond politely. He kisses me softly on the lips, smiling at me. I force a smile.

"Andrew, would you like anything?" Ben asks him.

"No Thank you, Senator." Andrew responds.

"I shall be right back." Ben tells us. I rub my wrist gently as it burns. Andrew walks closer to me, taking my wrist in his hand, he gazes down at it, and a red mark surfaces. He smiles, rubbing it gently.

Ben walks up carrying a glass of wine, he hands it to me.

"Here darling." He says, handing me the wine. "I am going to talk with Christian for a moment, will you be okay here by yourself?" Ben asks me. I nod my head and he walks away.

"Where's Kelly?" I ask Andrew. Andrew chuckles.

"I don't know, she went off somewhere." He responds to me.

"You don't know where your date is?" I ask him confused.

"She is free to do as she pleases. I put no restrictions on her." He tells me. I nod my head. Ben walks back over to us.

"Jenna, I have to stay for awhile. I think you should go home now. Come on, I'll walk you out." He explains to me. I turn to Andrew.

"Goodnight Andrew."

"Goodnight Jenna." He smiles and walks away. Ben takes my hand and we walk out to the front. He kisses me and places me in the limo and we drive away.

The limo drives into my driveway and I rush inside. I change into a pair of sweats and take a walk down to the cliff. I sit on the edge of the cliff, staring out at the lake.

"What are you doing out here this late by yourself?" I look up, and Andrew smiles as he sits next to me.

"What are you doing here?" I ask him.

"I followed you." He says to me. I smile at him. I stare back out at the lake.

"Where is Kelly?" I ask him with wonder. He laughs, shaking his head.

"Why are you so concerned about Kelly?" Andrew asks me, chuckling. He kicks the grass with his foot.

"It's the first girl I have ever seen you with. You two looked awfully cozy tonight." I respond with a smirk.

"I am like that with every girl that I take out."

"Do you really like her?"

"No. I am very shallow and self centered, and I'm incapable of acquiring any real feelings for a woman." He responds honestly. I laugh loudly at his comment.

"That is so funny."

"I'm happy I amuse you Jenna." Andrew says, smiling.

"Love and relationships aren't always bad, Andrew."

"I look at love as an addiction, and I don't like to be addicted to anything. Relationships to me are a form of slavery, it is a way of saying I am chained to this person. I like to do what I want, when I want, and I don't want to have to answer to anyone about anything." He explains in depth.

"My relationship is far from perfect. So I can't judge anyone." I tell him.

"Why do you stay it in it?"

"Because I vowed to honor, obey and love him forever."

"Why do have to honor and obey? Why can't you just love him forever?" I smile, looking down.

"Life isn't that simple, love isn't that simple."

"It should be." I nod my head.

I lie back on the grass, staring up at the sky. Andrew lies back next to me.

Andrew is very talkative and begins a conversation, telling me all about him. I learn that he is originally from New York, and moved here two years ago when his father opened a new firm. We sit silently and I fall asleep. I wake as Andrew lightly touches my shoulder. I sit up.

"We fell asleep; it's 3:00 am." He says to me. I stand up immediately; my heart beats so fast, I have to bend to catch my breath.

"Jenna, are you okay?" Andrew asks me. I stand upright.

"I have to go… I really have to go." I tell him. I start running. I run until I am walking through the back door. I creep in quietly. The house is silent and all the lights out, I exhale with relief.

"Where have you been?" I jump as Ben turns on a light and walks up to me.

"I went down to the cliff… I fell asleep." I tell him. He walks closer to me. Without warning, he back hands me, hitting me right in my eye, I fall to the ground.

"Liar!" He screams at me, his eyes blazing. I slide backwards on the tile and lean against the fridge, placing my hands up, frightened.

"I swear Ben… I swear!" I tell him tearfully. He grasps my wrist, pulling me up. He forcibly pulls me down the hallway to the bedroom; he throws me on the bed, and then walks to the bedroom door, locking it.

"Are you sleeping around on me?" he screams angrily.

"No… No!" I respond, frightened.

"You are mine, forever and always! Only mine!" he screams angrily.

His infuriation is so deep; he slides the gold-buckle, dark brown leather belt out of the loops of his pants, quickly hitting me without warning. His hits are close and fast, not even giving me a chance to catch my breath. He screams like a crazed lunatic.

"You're mine! You're fucking mine! Do you hear me? Mine… Only mine… Forever… Forever!" He screams. His violence inflames out of control as he hits my right calf over and over. I feel it tighten as it swells and he continues his relentless thrashing of the belt. The belt slides out of his hand, falling on the bed. He picks it up quickly, not realizing he had the gold buckle at the end. The gold buckle hits my calf once, and like a balloon my calf pops, splitting wide open all the way down to my ankle. I can feel the blood as it oozes out quickly down both sides of my calf. He hits it again and I feel something snap like a rubber band in my ankle. I scream and Ben stops, standing up, looking at my lacerated calf.

"Look what you made me do! Look what you made me do!" He screams angrily. He raises the belt again, hitting me in the lower back. The pain sears deeply through my skin like a hot iron as he continues. I lay helplessly on the bed, taking the punishment. He doesn't tire easily, and I can feel every part of my body burning as the bloody belt marks sear through me, and my mangled calf bleeds.

When he's finished he leaves the bedroom. I stare at the blank wall. A deep depression overwhelms me and my want to die grows stronger as the throbbing through my body is unbearable. I attempt to lift myself up, but the marks send stabbing pains through my muscles, weakening me, I fall back on the bed and sob.

I wake in the morning, and my body is stiff and cold. I cannot feel my right leg. I lie on my stomach, unable to move. Ben is gone and I am alone in a world of suffering and pain. My cell rings and I am unable to move to retrieve it.

For hours I lay still, staring at the blank wall. The bedroom door opens and my sister Christie rushes into the room with Manny. She looks down at my broken, naked body horrified. She places a sheet around me.

"Oh my God!" She says to me. She sits on the bed next to me. She attempts to move me, but I scream in pain. She begins to sob. Manny takes out his cell phone.

"I need an ambulance… Now!" He says frantically. The ambulance arrives immediately. Two men gently pick me up, placing me on my stomach on the gurney, and roll me away.

The emergency doctor examines me and admits me immediately. The cut on my right calf was so deep it severed my Achilles tendon. They took me into surgery to repair it. Christie waits with Manny in the waiting room while I am in surgery. Ben rushes into the waiting room with Rocco. Manny approaches him.

"You did this to her, didn't you!" Manny screams angrily.

"No, someone broke into the house." Ben responds quickly.

"How do you know someone broke into the house?" Manny asks Ben suspiciously.

"Because they stole all of our jewelry… I have a police report. I didn't realize Jenna was in the house, I left early this morning, and she was fine." Ben tells Manny. He hands Manny the police report. Manny gazes over the report and hands it back to Ben.

"The report was made after we found Jenna." Manny tells him madly.

"Of course it was, I didn't find out until they told me Jenna was in the hospital, so I went by the house and realized we had been robbed." Ben explains quickly.

"Why would you go by the house, when your wife is in the hospital? Shouldn't your first priority be to make sure your wife is okay?" Manny continues.

"I was distraught… I wasn't thinking." Ben answers nervously. Manny shakes his head, and sits down on the chair in the waiting room. Andrew walks into the waiting room, Ben stands up, shaking his hand.

"Thank you for coming on such short notice, Andrew."

"That is my job, Senator." Andrew responds. Christie walks up to Andrew.

"Hi Andrew." She says with a smile.

"Hi Christie." Andrew responds smiling.

"How do you two know each other?" Ben asks, confused. Christie stares at Andrew.

"Jenna and I were at the pub and Andrew was up there. It was just a hi and bye thing, you know, Ben?" Christie explains quickly. Manny smiles, and walks up to Andrew.

"You're the attorney." Manny says, still smiling.

"Yes." He responds. The doctor walks out to the waiting room.

"Jenna Kramer." They all walk up to him.

"Jenna Kramer is my wife, how is she?" Ben answers.

"Mr. Kramer, we were able to repair her Achilles tendon, and she will be in a cast for about 12 weeks. Now the belt marks on her back are pretty severe. We are using a special medicated crème to help them." The doctor explains.

"Belt marks?" Andrew asks confused.

"Yes. Mrs. Kramer was beaten badly by a belt." The doctor continues. Andrew nods his head.

"Can we see her?" Ben asks the doctor.

"Of course, follow me." He responds. He walks them down the hall, and to the Intensive Care Unit.

The nurse is placing crème on my back, exposing the bloody belt marks as they walk in. Andrew gasps as he sees them.

The nurse ties up my gown, then gently lays me flat.

"Are you comfortable?" the nurse ask me. I nod my head. Ben walks over, sitting on the chair in front of my bed.

"Darling." He says to me. I turn away from him, staring at the blank wall. My mind wanders to the dark place, where only I can go. Ben exhales and stands up. He looks at Andrew.

"I'm going to go get a cup of coffee. I will be right back." Ben tells him. Andrew nods his head. Christies sits down on the chair in front of my bed, stroking my head gently. Manny approaches Andrew.

"You and Jenna sure spend a lot of time together." Manny says to him. He stares at me.

"We're friends." Andrew responds.

"Why are you here, Andrew?"

"Ben asked me to be here. I'm his lawyer."

"I see." Andrew continues to stare at me with a look of worry in his eyes.

Chapter IV

My mind is sharp, but distraught, as I think of Ben's insidious abuse that had extended throughout our whole relationship. The tragedy and the devastation of the physical and emotional wounds I now and forever carried with me. Andrew stares at me with worry. Manny notices.

"You can go to talk to her, you know." Manny tells him. He nods and walks over to the bed. Christie stands up and walks over to Manny. Andrew sits down and gently places his hand on my arm, rubbing it lightly.

"Jenna." He says in a whisper. I turn and face him. He smiles at me and I smile back.

"Hi." I say to him softly.

"Hi."

"What are you doing here?" I ask him.

"Ben asked me to come."

"Oh."

"Are you okay?" he asks me worriedly.

"Yeah." Ben walks into the room. Andrew stands, and Ben walks over to the bed. I once again turn away, this time Manny notices. He approaches Ben.

"You did this to her, didn't you?" Manny says to him angrily.

"I don't know what you're talking about." Ben responds, gritting his teeth.

"Why won't she look at you, Ben?" Ben glares at Manny.

"Jenna, Ben did this to you, didn't he." I don't answer. My silence only acknowledges Manny's accusation, it angers him deeply and he lunges towards Ben, Andrew restrains him.

"You son of a bitch, I know you did this! I know you hurt her!" He screams madly.

"Calm down, Manny!" Andrew tells him.

"He did this to her Andrew! I know he did!" Manny says tearfully. Andrew turns to look at Ben, and Ben looks down.

"You have no proof." Andrew responds.

"The mark she bares on her back are proof enough, aren't they?" Manny asks him with desperation.

"I don't know what you mean." Andrew says to him confused.

"I guarantee if you compare his belt to her back, it will match!" Andrew walks over to Ben.

"Can I see your belt?" Andrew asks him.

"No." Ben answers quickly.

"Why not?" Andrew asks Ben.

"I refuse to submit to Manny's outlandish accusations."

"You can put his accusations to rest by giving me your belt." Andrew tells him strongly.

"No. I won't." Andrew exhales and walks back over to Manny.

"His refusal is just more proof that he did it!" Manny tells him. Ben's cell rings and he walks out of the room, answering it.

Andrew sits back down on the chair next to my bed.

"Jenna." He says softly. I turn to him.

"Did Ben do this to you?" he asks me calmly.

Tears fill my eyes and I turn away, facing the blank wall. He lightly rubs my shoulder, and I turn back to face him.

"It's okay, you can tell me." Andrew says to me softly. I stare up at Christie and Manny.

"I can't." I whisper.

"Are you afraid?" I nod my head. He smiles at me.

"I promise, I won't let anyone hurt you. You can trust me, Jenna." I did trust him. We stare at each other for a moment, smiling.

"Yes. Ben did this." I tell him distraught.

My acknowledgment of the abuse from Ben throws Manny into a rage. He rushes out of the room, searching for Ben, who is standing down the hall, talking on his cell. He clenches his fist and hits Ben in the face, he catches him off guard, and Ben's cell flies in the air, smashing to the floor. Andrew rushes out of the room and grabs Manny, restraining him.

"Don't do this!" Andrew says to him.

"You son of bitch, you put your hands on her! I am going to kill you!" Manny screams. Rocco is sitting in the waiting room. Manny's yelling catches his attention and he runs up, standing protectively in front of Ben. Ben retrieves a handkerchief from his pocket and wipes his bleeding lip.

"I'm going to sue you!" He says madly to Manny.

"You had better hope I don't get loose, cause if I do there will be nothing fucking left of you!" Manny screams, enraged.

"Senator, I think it would be better if you left." Andrew tells him calmly.

"I am not leaving my wife, Andrew."

"I am your attorney, and I am telling you it is in your best interest to leave this hospital, now!" Andrew explains to him. Ben nods his head and turns, walking way with Rocco in tow.

I lie on the bed sobbing as I hear Manny screaming outside my room. Christies embraces me, holding me close. Andrew and

Manny walk into the room a few minutes later. Christie releases me and walks over to Manny, embracing him tightly. Andrew sits on the chair next to my bed.

"I am going to call the police and have them come up here so you can tell them what happened." Andrew explains to me. I shake my head.

"No Andrew, I can't tell them."

"Why not?"

"Because, I can't do that to Ben." Manny pulls away from Christie and walks over to the side of my bed.

"Look what he did to you; you can't let him get away with that." Manny says to me madly.

"Manny, I won't do it."

"Jenna, he is a criminal, he needs to be in jail. He needs to pay for what he did to you!" I shake my head, and Manny exhales.

"It was an accident. He was just very angry." I tell Manny.

"He accidently hit you a hundred times with a belt?" Manny asks me sarcastically.

"It was my fault."

"How was it your fault?" Manny asks, astounded.

"I fell asleep at the cliff and didn't get home till 3:00 a.m." I tell Manny. Andrew interjects.

"Wait. This happened after we were at the cliff?" Andrew asks me.

"Yes." Andrew shakes his head and looks down. "He just lost control, he didn't mean it." I continue.

"Oh my God, I can't believe you are sticking up for him!" Manny says with disbelief.

"Jenna, are you sure you don't want me to call the police?" Andrew asks me.

"No. Andrew, please don't." I tell him. He nods his head and stands up. Manny walks closer to me.

"You're not going home with him!" Manny says to me sternly.

"He's my husband, I have to." I tell him distraught. He sits down on the chair and takes my hand in his.

"No, you don't, you can come home with me and Christie." Manny says softly.

"Manny, I'm not leaving Ben over one incident."

"I'm positive this isn't the first incident." He snaps.

"I'm not doing it, so you can stop talking about it!" I snap back. Manny stands up, and stomps out of the room.

I stay the night at the hospital, and Ben drives me home the following morning. We don't discuss the beating, we never discussed the beatings.

As we drive up in the driveway, Rocco grasps my crutches from the trunk and hands them to me as he opens the door. I crutch into the house and to the bedroom. I hobble to the bed, lying down. Ben walks into the bedroom, sitting on the bed. I glare at him.

"I'm sorry Jenna. I didn't mean to hurt you that bad." He says to me, distraught. I nod my head politely, but his apology does not comfort me. He stands up and walks out of the bedroom. My cell buzzes and it's a text from Andrew.

"Jenna." He texts.

"Yes."

"Are you home from the hospital yet?"

"Yes. I just got home."

"How are you feeling?"

"A little sore, but not too bad."

"That's good. Ben's not hurting you or anything like that?"

"No. Everything is fine."

"I was just checking up on you. Are you going to work tomorrow?"

"Yes."

"I'll see you tomorrow then."

"Ok see you tomorrow."
Manny was insistent on driving me to work every day. He wanted to keep a close eye on me; mostly it was his way of keeping a close eye on Ben.

He drives into my driveway and steps out of the car. Ben is walking to the limo. Manny glares at him as he passes by, without a word. He walks into the house, and I am sitting at the dining room table. I smile as I see him.

"Hi." I say with a big grin on my face.

"Hi. Are you ready to go?" Manny asks nicely. I nod my head. I retrieve my crutches and hobble out to the car.

We leave the house and drive towards the office. Manny turns down the radio.

"Your pedophile husband called Christie this morning, he's going out of town for a few days, so you will be staying with us."

"Okay." I respond, smiling. We pull up in front of the office. Manny steps out of the car and retrieves my crutches from the back seat. He helps me out of the car, and I place the crutches under my arms. He kisses me on the forehead with a smile.

"Have a good day." Manny says to me pleasantly.

"You too." I respond to him. I crutch up to the sidewalk and Manny leaves. The cement is cracked, and I struggle as I hobble across it. I catch one of my crutches in one of the cracks and lose my balance, I begin to fall, and as the inevitable crash is about to occur, I feel arms around me. I stare up and Andrew cradles me in his arms.

"Thank you." I say to him.

"No problem." He responds with a smile. He turns to Eric. "Grab her crutches." Andrew tells him. Eric nods and picks my crutches up from the ground as Andrew carries me into the office.

Andrew places me down on a chair in the conference room. Kathleen walks in.

"Jenna, we are moving your computer down to the conference room so you don't have to climb the stairs." Kathleen tells me sweetly.

"Ok. Thank you." I respond to her. She walks closer, kneeling next to me.

"I'm sorry Ben did this to. If you ever need anything, just ask okay?" She whispers. I am surprised by her comment, I nod my head. She pats my knee, smiling, and leaves. Andrew walks over to me.

"Can I get you a cup of coffee?" he asks me.

"How does Kathleen know that Ben did this to me?" I ask Andrew.

"Manny told her. He thought that it would help keep Ben out of the office, but Franklin said he wouldn't get involved." Andrew answers.

"How do you know that Manny told her?" I ask him.

"Because Manny called me and told me he did."

"How did he get your number?" My many questions bring the impatience out of Andrew. He kneels next to my chair.

"Manny is protecting you the best he knows how. That's all." He says simply. I nod my head and he stands up. "So, can I get you a cup of coffee?"

"Yeah." I respond.

I work for four hours, and my neck and back begin to ache from sitting so long. I move my head side to side, and attempt to stretch. Andrew walks over to me.

"What's wrong?" he asks me.

"My back and neck ache." I tell him. He places his hands on my neck and massages it gently. I close my eyes.

"Feel better?" he asks as he gently kneads his fingers across my neck.

"Mhm." He moves his hands to my back and rubs it gently.

"Oh." I moan as he hits the right spot. I become relaxed. Andrew leans to my ear.

"You like that, huh." He whispers seductively.

"It feels so good." I respond with my eyes closed.

He places gentle kisses on my neck as he massages my back. I am aroused instantly. I turn placing my lips to his pulling him close.

The slamming of the conference room door interrupts us.

"Are you two crazy, you want to get busted or something?" Eric says to us worriedly.

"Sorry." I respond instantly.

"I'm not." Andrew says with a smirk.

Eric walks to the conference door, opening as he shakes his head. Andrew stares at me and I smile. Without warning, he scoops me into his arms.

"Let's get out of here." He says with a smile.

"I can't leave work." I tell him.

"Yes. You can you have a doctor's appointment." He says with a quick wink. I nod my head, and he walks me out to the front door, setting me down on the step.

"I'm going to go tell Kathleen." He says to me he runs up the steps. Andrew runs down the steps a few minutes later. He scoops me into his arms.

"Time to go." He says with a smile.

"My crutches." I tell him.

"You don't need them." He opens the door and we leave. Andrew places me in the passenger seat of his car, and we drive out of the parking lot. He drives towards my house and I look at him, confused. I smile as he drives into the cliff parking lot.

He retrieves a blanket from his backseat, and then opens my door, scooping me into his arms, and carrying me to the cliff. He sits me down, and then lays the blanket out. I scoot over to it. I lie down, closing my eyes, letting the sun shine down on my face. Andrew lies next to me. He places his arm around me, pulling me close to him. The smell of the lake air fills my senses, bringing an instant smile to my face. I exhale.

"It's such a nice day." I say aloud.

"I know, too nice to be stuck in an office all day." Andrew states.

We stay for a little while longer, and then Andrew drives back to his house. He carries me inside, and the place is trashed. I look around with disgust.

"What happened?" I ask him confused.

"It's always like this."

"Oh."

"I think this is the first time you have been over sober." He tells me. I laugh.

"Oh yeah." I respond, smiling. He places me on the couch and sits down next to me.

"Let's make out." He says out of the blue. I chuckle.

He places his lips to mine kissing me softly. I clutch his back, pulling him closer. He lies down, pulling me down with him, cuddling me close.

"I'm so addicted to you Jenna." He says breathlessly. I gasp at his comment.

"I'm addicted to you too." I respond.

We laze around talking, kissing, and just enjoying time alone together. My cell phone rings. I grasp my purse from the side of the couch and answer it.

"Hello." I answer.

"Jenna, it's Manny. I'm running a few minutes late. I will be there as soon as I can." He says to me.

"I'm not at work."

"Where are you?"

"I'm at Andrew's."

"Let me talk to him." I hand my cell to Andrew.

"It's Manny." I say to him. He takes the cell.

"Hello… yeah… I'll bring her home… yeah… okay… bye." Andrew hands me my cell back, and I place it in my purse. He cuddles me close.

"Is he coming here to pick me up?" I ask him.

"No. I'm going to drive you there later." Andrew responds. I nod my head. I sit up.

"What's wrong?" Andrew asks me.

"I'm hungry." I tell him.

"You want me to order some take out?" he asks me.

"No. I can cook something." I stand, and hobble on my cast to the kitchen. Andrew follows.

"Jenna. I don't think you're supposed to walk on your foot." He says to me worriedly.

"The doctor said it's a walking cast, which means I can walk on it." I gaze through the fridge and retrieve parmesan cheese, heavy whipping cream, butter, and broccoli. Andrew walks into the kitchen.

"What are you making?" he asks me. I search through the cabinet, and am surprised to find Fettuccine noodles. I place them on the counter.

"Fettuccine Alfredo." I tell him. He smiles.

"Can I help you?" he asks me.

"No. Get out of the kitchen." I respond, playfully pushing him.

"Ok." He says, throwing his hands in the air.

I prepare the sauce then wait for the water to boil for the noodles. I sit on the counter top, and Andrew walks into the kitchen. He turns the burners off then walks over, scooping me into his arms.

"Andrew. I am making food." I say to him. He carries me into the bedroom, laying me on the bed.

"Its play time." He says, smirking.

After we make love, I dress and hobble into the kitchen. I turn the burners back on, reheating the sauce and boiling the water. I place the noodles in the pot and stir them quickly. Andrew walks in behind me, wrapping his arms around me, kissing my neck softly. I dip the ladle into the sauce, and place it in his mouth.

"How does it taste?" I ask him.

"Good. Really good." He responds happily.

The front door opens, Eric and Matt walk in.

"What smells so good?" Eric asks as he walks into the kitchen.

"Jenna is cooking." Andrew responds.

"Is there enough for all of us? I'm starving." Matt says.

"Yes, there is plenty." I tell him.

"I'll make a salad!" Eric offers. He walks to the fridge and takes out the ingredients he needs, and then prepares the salad. Matt sets the table. I mix the noodles in the sauce then I hobble to the table, placing the pot down. We all sit and eat.

"This is really good, Jenna." Eric says as he takes another of bite from his plate.

"Thank you." I tell him. We finish eating then retire in the living room watching television. I cuddle close to Andrew. I fall asleep almost instantly. Andrew smiles as he stares down at me. My cell rings and he retrieves it. Manny is calling.

"Hello." Andrew answers.

"Andrew. Are you bringing Jenna home soon? It's getting late." Manny asks him.

"She's asleep right now. I really don't want to wake her."

"So is she staying there tonight?"

"If you don't mind?"

"I don't mind if it's okay with you. I trust you."

"Ok. She will just stay. I can drive her to work in the morning." He says to Manny.

"Cool. I'll talk to you later."

"Bye." Andrew hangs up my cell and places it in my purse. He finishes watching the movie then carries me into the bedroom, laying me on the bed. He undresses me and places one of his t-shirts on me, then wraps his arms around me, cuddling me close.

I wake in the morning to my leg throbbing. I sit up and place my hand on my cast.

"Ohhh!" I grimace. Andrew sits up.

"Hey." Andrew says as he sits up.

"My leg hurts." I tell him.

"Where are your pain pills?" he asks me.

"In my purse." I answer. He stands up and walks out to the living room, retrieving my purse. He grabs a bottle of water from the fridge and walks back into the bedroom with my purse; he takes out a bottle of pain pills and my birth control pills.

"Which one?" he asks me, confused.

"Both of them." I tell him. He nods and hands me the bottle of pain pills and my packet of birth control pills. I pop the birth control pill through the foil back. Andrew stares at me.

"Pain pills come in a pack?" he asks me.

"There not pain pills; they're my birth control pills." I tell him casually.

A look of surprise encompasses his face. I open the pain pills and take two pills out and wash them down with the bottled water. Andrew walks over, sitting next to me.

"You never told me you were on birth control." He says to me.

"You never asked."

"I'm glad I know, because now I can stop using condoms."

"No you can't. You're supposed to use both. Ben and I do."

"You and your husband use condoms even though you're on birth control pills?" he asks me, astounded.

"Yes. Ben doesn't want any children. So he is super careful."

"You are probably better off using them with him, being as he sleeps around so much. But I'm not using them with you anymore." He says sarcastically.

"Yes you are, you sleep around too."

"No I don't. Since I have been intimate with you I haven't been with another woman."

"Really?" I ask him surprised.

"Really. You take care of my needs." He says provocatively. He bends his head, placing a sweet kiss on my lips. I smile at him.

My cell buzzing interrupts us. And I retrieve it from my purse and gaze at it. I have five new voicemails, all from Ben. I place my phone on speaker and listen to it.

"Darling it's me, call me back."

"Jenna, I have already left one voicemail where are you? Please call me back."

"Jenna this is your husband. I am demanding that you call me back now!"

"Damn it Jenna. Where are you? I'm getting very impatient!" he says madly.

"I am tracing your phone, right now!" A knock at the front door makes me jump. Andrew jumps out of the bed and rushes to the door.

"Where is my wife?" Ben asks madly as he pushes his way through the door.

"She is not here. If you don't mind I would like you to leave my house, now!" Andrew tells Ben sternly. Eric and Matt rush out of the room and stand behind Andrew.

"I want my wife!" Ben screams.

"She's not here!" Matt tells him.

"You're lying, I traced her phone here." Ben says to them.

"Oh, that. Jenna left her phone at the office when she left yesterday. I didn't want anyone to steal it, so I brought it home with me. I was going to give it to her today." Andrew explains as he hands my cell to Ben. Ben smiles at him.

"Thank you. I apologize for my disruption." He says to Andrew.

"No problem." Andrew responds. Ben leaves.

Andrew walks back into the bedroom and sits down on the bed. I look at him, frightened.

"I'm in so much trouble." He embraces me.

"No. It will be fine."

Andrew and I get ready for work and leave. We drive to the office; we didn't want to risk being seen together, so Andrew drops me off in front of the building before he heads to the parking lot. I hobble inside.

Ben is sitting at the dining room table when I walk into the kitchen. I exhale as I hobble over to him sitting down.

"Where have you been?" he asks me.

"I was at Christies." I tell him.

"Why haven't you called me?"

"I lost my phone." I tell him. He nods and reaches into his pocket and hands me my cell.

"Come on, we're going home. I already talked to Franklin." He says to me. I nod my head and stand up, hobbling into the conference room, retrieving my purse. I gaze at Andrew and he smiles.

My momentary disappearance frightened Ben, so he kept me close to him, not allowing me any access outside of the house. He made me take time off from work to heal my leg. Andrew and I kept in contact via text.

"I finally got my cast off." I text him.

"That's great."

"Yeah. I limp when I walk, but it doesn't really hurt anymore."

"That's good."

"I miss working."

"I miss you." I smile at his text.

"I miss you too."

"It's seems like forever since I've seen you."

"I know."

"When do you think you will be able to get out?"

"I don't know, Andrew. Ben hasn't been traveling, and if he's not with me, Rocco is. It's because I went missing for a day, that's what he said. He is very paranoid right now."

"I really want to see you."

"I want to see you too." I hear Ben's shoes as they hit the wood floor walking down the hallway.

"I have to go Ben is home. I'll text you later."

It was Saturday, Ben and I had plans to attend a golf outing for charity. I stare through the pamphlet advertisements of donators and see Carington Associates as one of the major contributors. I smile as I see Andrews name beneath Williams. I dress in a strapless, form-fitting, white summer dress, with a large white brim hat. I wear matching high heel sandals. I pin my hair up and finish my makeup and walk out to the living room, where Ben is sitting, waiting for me. He walks up to me, smiling.

"I have something for you that will go perfectly with that dress and your eyes." He says to me with a smile.

He reaches into his pocket and takes out a red velvet jewelry box. He opens it and inside is an emerald diamond necklace, with a matching bracelet and earrings. He must have started a new affair, I assume, since his trips switched from New Hampshire to Maine. That must be where his new lover lives. I was surprisingly happy; it meant he would leave me alone.

"It's beautiful." I tell him. I close the box and set it down on the kitchen table. He embraces me and nuzzles his face in my hair.

"Not as beautiful as you are." He states. "Turn around, and I will put it on." He says to me. I turn, and he gently clasps the necklace. I put the earrings in my ears, and Ben clasps the bracelet on me. He gazes at me proudly.

"Are you ready to go?" he asks me.

"Yes." I respond to him.

It was beautiful summer day. The smell of tulips and fresh cut grass fill my senses. My leg tired easily as we continued to walk around, I sit for a moment as Ben talked with a crowd of people. He walks over to me a few minutes later.

"Darling, let's go." Ben says, interrupting my tranquil state. I stand up and he places his hand in mine, and we walk over to where they are playing golf. Ben despised golf; he felt it was a waste of time and money. But he found it imperative to at least watch those that were playing. We sit on chairs near the first hole. The breeze kicks up and my hat flies off my head. With natural impulse, I jump up and chase it down. Each time I would bend it would float back up in the air. I run about a hundred feet until I finally catch it. I smile proudly as I lift it up, placing it on my head.

"Jenna." I turn and Andrew smiles as he walks up, followed by his parents.

"Hi Andrew!" I respond, staring at him with endearing eyes. He walks closer to me. I want to throw my arms around him so badly, but Ben is too close.

"You look like your getting around pretty good." Andrew tells me.

"Yeah. My leg feels so much lighter without that big cast!" I tell him.

Ben walks up; he extends his hand to William.

"William old buddy, how are you?" Ben asks him.

"I'm great. It is so good to see you Ben." William tells him.

"Hi Jenna!" William says sweetly.

"Hi William." I respond. A small petite woman with Andrew's eyes walks closer to us.

"Wendy." Ben says as he kisses her on the cheek. Ben drapes his arm around me. "Wendy, this is my wife Jenna." He says to her.

"Jenna, it is so nice to meet you." Wendy says as she shakes my hand.

"It's very nice to meet you too." I tell her. Ben and William walk away, talking.

"They are so rude." Wendy says to me. She places her arm in mine and we walk, Andrew follows.

"So Jenna, how old are you?" Wendy asks me.

"22." She stops and looks at me, astounded.

"You are too young to be a Senators wife." I turn to Andrew and begin to laugh.

"What is so funny?" Wendy asks confused.

"Nothing mother." Andrew responds.

"You must have been awfully young when you married. How old were you?" she asks me. I laugh again. She definitely was Andrew's mother.

"She was 18 and still a senior in high school. She married in March and graduated in June." Andrew explains quickly. His memory brings a smile to my face. I smile at him and he smiles back. Wendy stares at Andrew, then at me. She places her arm in mine and walks, Andrew follows.

"Your parents… They were okay with this marriage?"

"My mother passed away when I was 12. My father left me with my sister. She and her husband raised me."

"Oh dear! You poor thing!" Wendy says, disconcerted. Ben walks up with William.

"Can I have my wife back, Wendy?" Ben asks with a grin.

"I suppose." Wendy responds jokingly. Ben places his hand in mine.

"Come on, darling; let's go finish watching grown men get excited about hitting small balls in small holes." He states with a chuckle.

"Do you mind if I accompany the both of you?" William asks us.

"It would be our pleasure." Ben responds nicely. We walk away. I turn to look at Andrew, and he is standing staring at me. Wendy interrupts his gaze, placing her arm in his, walking.

"Andrew, what is your relationship with Jenna?" his mother asks him.

"We are friends." He tells her. She stops and stares into his eyes.

"Friends? I see the way you look at her and the way she looks at you, you are way more than friends." She says to him.

"We spend time together."

"Spend time together?"

"It's no big deal, mother."

"Ben Kramer is a very powerful and dangerous man, not a man you want on your bad side."

"I know what I'm doing, mother."

"All I'm asking you to do is to be careful."

"I promise you I will be careful." She smiles and they walk.

Ben and William walk over and watch the golfers. I stand waiting, Andrew walks up to me.

"I missed you." He whispers.

"I missed you too." I tell him

"You look very pretty today."

"Thank you." I respond to him. He places his hand on my thigh and slowly slides it to my garter, tugging lightly on it.

"Always sexy underneath." I tap his hand.

"Stop." I say nervously. He chuckles.

"There is a horse stable to the right of us, meet me there in fifteen minutes." He says with seriousness.

"I can't, I'm with Ben."

"Find a way. I will be there waiting for you." He smiles and walks away. Ben and William walk up to me.

"Darling, William and I are going to go watch them play on the tenth hole, would you like to go?" Ben asks me.

"How long will you be gone?" I ask him.

"How many holes are they playing?" Ben asks William

"18." William answers.

"Probably an hour and a half." Ben tells me.

"I'll wait here then." I tell him. He kisses me quickly.

"I'll see you in a little while." I nod and he walks away with William. They walk over to a golf cart and drive away. I wait until they are out of sight, and rush to the barn. I walk in the door and look around.

"I'm up here." Andrew says to me. I look up and he is standing atop the loft. I walk over to the ladder and slowly walk up it. As I reach the last step, Andrew helps me up. He wraps his arms around me.

"I knew you would come." He says as he grasps the hat from my head, throwing it the ground. He takes the pins out of my hair. My hair falls softly to the middle of my back. He places his hands on my face, staring into my eyes.

"I missed you so much, Jenna." He says with endearing eyes.

He places his lips to mine and I embrace him tightly. He scoops me into his arms, and places me gently down on the hay.

We make love. I lay on his chest as he runs his hand softly up my bare back. I lift my head.

"Can I ask you a very personal question?" Andrew asks me out of the blue. I lift my head and look at him.

"Of course."

"It's been over three weeks. Have you been intimate with Ben?" He asks me nervously. I stroke his head gently.

"No." He smiles.

I kiss him softly on the lips. He stares into my eyes, exhaling.

I stand up, and quickly dress, and pin my hair up.

"I have to go, Ben will be back any minute."

"Okay." He responds. I walk over to the ladder.

"Jenna." Andrew blurts out.

"Yes." I respond, turning to him. He exhales and stares.

"Nothing. I'll see you a little bit."

"Okay."

Chapter V

The wind was picking up, I hold my hat with my hand as I scurry to the spot I had been before. I made it just in time; five minutes later, Ben shows up. He wraps his arm around me, kissing me quickly. He stares at me strangely. He lifts his hand and takes a piece of hay out of my hair.

"Where did that come from?" he asks me confused. William walks up.

"There is hay everywhere. It's windy, I'm sure it flew into her hair." William says quickly. Ben smiles, nodding his head and Andrew walks up, arm in arm with Wendy.

"Did you boys have fun?" Wendy asks them. William glares at Andrew.

"Yes it was very enjoyable. I am exhausted. I think we will call it a day." Ben says to them. We say our goodbyes and leave. William approaches Andrew. He takes a piece of hay from his hair.

"Jenna had the exact same hay in her hair." William says to him. Andrew looks down. "What are you doing, son?"

"I know what I'm doing father."

"I don't think you do. She is married to a Senator. For the love of God! Do you know how dangerous this affair you're having is? Ben Kramer is a very jealous and dangerous man. You are not only risking yourself, but you are also risking Jenna." William explains to him angrily.

"I am an adult, what I do is none of your concern." Andrew responds madly. He turns and walks away. William and Wendy follow behind him.

"Don't walk away from me, son!" William says to him. He stops and turns to him.

"I am not going to stop seeing her! You can yell till you are blue in the face!" Andrew tells him defensively. William walks closer to him, staring into his eyes.

"You're in love with her." William says, gasping. Andrew looks at him, distraught.

"No… I-I just enjoy being with her." He responds stuttering.

"I love you son, I don't want to see you get hurt."

"I am not going to get hurt father, I promise you." William realizes that he cannot win this argument with Andrew, so he surrenders.

"Okay Son." William says, as he pats him on the shoulder.

Ben and I drive home; he receives a call on his cell.

"Yes… I can be on a plane tonight… Okay… See you soon." Ben hangs up his cell and turns to me.

"I have to go to Maine tonight; the Senator there wants to go over the proposal."

"Okay."

He drapes his arm around me, kissing me softly on the cheek.

"I will miss you."

"I will miss you too." I respond. He bends his head slightly, kissing me softly on the lips.

I sit on the bed as Ben rushes around the room packing.

"Can I stay at Christies while you're gone?" I ask him.

"If you would like." He answers.

"I want to."

"Okay." He walks over to the bed and sits next to me. He takes my hand in his, and plays with my fingers.

"I promise, when I get back, we will plan a trip away, just you and I." he tells me. I smile, nodding my head.

"I love you, Jenna." He says emotionally. He embraces me tightly.

"I love you too." I respond. He kisses me quickly and stands, grasping his suitcase.

"See you soon darling." He rolls his suitcase and leaves.

I drive to Christie's house; I use my key and walk into the house.

Christie and Manny were at a function for Manny's job. I sit on the couch, watching television. My cell buzzes. I retrieve it and it's a text from Andrew.

"What are you doing?" he text.

"Waiting for Christie to get home."

"You are not with Ben?"

"No, Ben is out of town, I'm staying with my Christie."

"Oh. We are having a few friends over, you should come by."

"I don't know."

"I would really like to see you… Do you remember how to get to my house?"

"No not at all."
"Here is my address: 333 Plintkon Avenue. I expect you here within the hour."

"You are awfully pushy."

"It's only because I want to see you." His text brings a smile to my face.

"Okay. I have to shower first."

"See you soon."

I take a quick shower and stare at my clothes in the closet. I pick out a black tank top and dark jeans. I pair it off with a pair of black knee boots. I wear my hair down and straight iron it. I finish my makeup and leave.

I drive to the address Andrew had given me, there are cars everywhere. I park down the street and walk up the sidewalk. As I reach his driveway, my nerves get the best of me and I turn around, walking back towards my car.

"Jenna." Andrew screams as he walks down the sidewalk. I stop and he walks up to me.

"Hi."

"Were you leaving?" he asks me.

"Yeah, kind of. I don't know. I feel a little uncomfortable being here." He drapes his arm around me.

"Don't feel uncomfortable. I assure you that you will have a good time. Come on lets go in." I nod my head and we walk into the house. Eric approaches me instantly. He hugs me, and then, with his hands still on my shoulders, he gazes at me.

"Wow, you look great!" He says to me.

"Thanks." I gaze around the house, and there are people scattered everywhere. Andrew approaches me.

"Do you want something to drink?" he asks me. I nod my head, smiling. Andrew hands me a drink, and then walks over to talk to a few of his friends. A man approaches me, smiling. His hair is longer and light brown.

"Hi, I'm Mark." He says to me, extending his hand out.

"Hi. I'm Jenna." I respond to him.

"I have never seen you at one of Andrew's party. How do you know him?" Mark asks me.

"He's my attorney." I tell him.

"I see." Mark responds. I talk with Mark for a little while longer, and then I walk through the house, searching for Andrew. Eric walks by, and I stop him.

"Where's Andrew?" I ask him.

"I don't know. Maybe he went to his bedroom." Eric responds.

I nod my head and walk to Andrew's bedroom. I open the door and its pitch black, so I turn on the light. I stand shocked, as I see Kelly lying on top of Andrew, kissing him.

"Jenna!" Andrew says immediately. I turn the light off, close the door, and walk out of the room. Confusion fills my head, and I walk without direction. Andrew rushes out of the bedroom as I reach the front door.

"Jenna, it wasn't what it looked like." He says to me nervously.

"Andrew, you don't owe me an explanation." I respond with a smile.

"Jenna, I was sleeping. She came in there… She kissed me, but I didn't kiss her back."

"Really Andrew, it's no big deal."

"Please let me talk to you." I search my mind for an excuse. I was smiling on the outside, but hurting on the inside. Talking to him would just reveal that, and I didn't want him to feel guilty. How could I? I was a married woman after all.

"Manny called, he really wants to talk to me. So I have to really go, we can talk later, okay?" I open the door and rush out before he could answer. The hurt fills me quickly as my heart reveals itself.

I run to my car as the tears stream down my face like a broken faucet. I frantically rummage through my purse too quickly and it falls from my hands, and the contents fly everywhere. I plummet to the ground, sobbing uncontrollably.

After a few minutes, I gather up all the contents on the ground and place them back in my purse. I open the car door and step in. I stare at Andrew's house as I start the car.

The devastation I felt was worse than I had ever felt from the beatings Ben had ensued upon me. That's when I realized; between the closet, the conference room and his, bedroom, I had fallen hopelessly in love with Andrew. I place my car in drive and drive away.

I drive into Christie's driveway, and shut off my car. I sit and stare out at the garage door. My cell buzzes, and I retrieve it from my purse.

"Jenna." Andrew texts.

"Yes?"

"Are you at Christies?" he asks me.

"Yes." My cell rings and I answer it.

"Andrew." I say simply.

"Do you mind if I come over and talk to you?" he asks me.

"Andrew, it's not necessary."

"Please Jenna."

"Andrew, you are free to be with who you want. So please don't make a big deal out of what happened tonight."

"I just really would feel better if we talked."

"I really have to go. I will see you at work on Monday."

"Jenna, please." Andrew pleads.

"Bye, Andrew." I hang up my cell and walk into the house.

I walk to the bedroom and ready myself for bed. I slide into the bed and curl to my pillow, thinking of Andrew.

I wake early, but laze around in the bed, staring at the blank wall, thinking of Andrew. A simple affair had become so complicated. Ad now, it was not only his body I desired, it was also his heart. How selfish of me to want more from him than I deserved.

The bedroom door opens, and Christie walks in.

"Hey, Andrew is here." She says to me. I sit up instantly.

"I don't want to see him." I tell Christie.

"Why not?" Andrew asks as he walks into the bedroom.

"Andrew." He gazes at Christie, and she leaves, closing the bedroom door. Andrew walks over the bed, sitting next to me.

"I have been calling you all morning." He says to me.

"I just woke up. I haven't even checked my phone yet." I tell him.

He rummages through my purse, and retrieves my cell phone, handing it to me. I stare down at it and there is a voicemail from his number. I look up at him.

"Listen to it." He says to me. I nod my head and retrieve the voicemail.

"Hi Jenna it's Andrew. I have never been really good at talking about my how I feel, but I really think it's imperative that I tell you.

Last night, when you left I had this unbelievable pain in my chest. I felt as if I couldn't breathe, like someone knocked the wind out of me. My mind was so confused, and the only thought I had, was that I had lost you. It was the most devastating thought I had ever had…"he exhales lightly. "It's when I realized somewhere between the closet, the conference room, my bedroom, I fell in love with you… I love you Jenna." The voicemail ends and I place my cell on the bed and look down.

"Jenna." Andrew says in a whisper. Tears fill my eyes as I look up at him.

"I, uh." I swallow hard as I stare at him. He waits patiently for me to speak. "I love you too." I say to him emotionally.

He embraces me tightly and I hold him close. He kisses me softly on the lips.

"I need you, Jenna." He says as he softly brushes the hair from my face.

"I need you too, Andrew." He holds me close.

"Can I take you home with me?" he asks with a smirk.

"Mhm." I respond.

He stands up, and I stand next to him, he places his hand in mine and we walk out to the living room. Christie and Manny smile at us.

"Have fun!" Is all Manny said. Andrew and I leave, and drive to his house.

The house is still filled with people from the night before. I walk around, attempting to tidy up as Andrew talks to a few of the people. I hang out for awhile and have a few drinks. As night falls, I walk into the kitchen and begin cleaning the dishes. Eric approaches me.

"Hey Jenna."

"Hi Eric."

"You want a drink?" he asks me, as he makes a Captain Morgan and coke.

"No. I'm good." I respond to him. He nods his head and walks away with his drink. I rinse the dishes and place them in the dishwasher. Andrew walks up behind me, wrapping his arms around me.

"You don't have to do that." He says to me.

"Andrew, your house is trashed."

"It's a bachelor pad. It's supposed to be messy." He says as he gently kisses my neck.

A fight breaks out in the living room, and Andrew releases me, running to break it up. I place the last dish in the dishwasher and close it. I walk out to the living room, and a girl is hitting Andrew as he restrains her boyfriend. I rush up to her.

"Stop hitting him." I scream as I grab her by the arm, pulling her away. She clenches her fist and attempts to punch me and misses, I clench my fist and punch her in the face, knocking her to the ground. She stands up and grabs my hair, pulling me to the ground. We wrestle on the carpet, and I manage to roll on top of her. I punch her again and again until I am pulled off of her.

"Easy, Rocky!" Andrew says with a chuckle as he pulls me off the girl. I shake my head. Eric walks over to help the girl up and she hits him. I pull away from Andrew, and grab her by the arm.

"You stupid bitch! Stop hitting everyone!" I yell at her. She stands up and attempts to hit me again. I forcibly march her to the door wall, throwing her out of it. I close and lock the door. Andrew and Eric walk over to me, laughing.

"You kicked her ass, Jenna." Eric says, still laughing. Andrew drapes his arm around me. He kisses me quickly on the lips.

"Come on baby, let's go to bed." He says simply. I nod and we walk to the bedroom.

I undress, wearing a light blue camisole and matching panties. I slide into the bed. Andrew undresses down to his boxers and slides next to me, he kisses me quickly and wraps his arms around me, pulling me close. I close my eyes and fall fast asleep.

My pounding head wakes me early. I only had drank a few drinks, but ended up with this unbelievable hangover. I sit up, holding my head.

"Ohhhh!" I grimace. Andrew sits up beside me.

"Headache." He asks grinning.

"Mhm." My stomach starts to twirl. I jump out of the bed and rush to the bathroom. I pick up the toilet seat and vomit all that is in my stomach. Andrew kneels next to me, holding my hair and rubbing my back. After I am finished I lie on the tile floor.

"Oh God. I'm dying." I say dramatically. Andrew chuckles. My body is so hot it feels like it's on fire, I slide my camisole off.

"Jenna, what are you doing?" Andrew says to me, astounded.

"Andrew you have seen me naked many times." He leaves the bathroom and comes back with a t-shirt. He kneels next to me helping me to a sitting position. He then slides the t-shirt on me. I lie back on the tile and he laughs.

"You can't sleep here." He says, still laughing.

"I'm going to die here." I tell him grimacing. He scoops me into his arms and carries me back to his bed, lying me down.

"I'll get you some aspirin." He says. I nod my head and curl to the pillow. Andrew walks back into his room and I am fast asleep. He slides back into the bed, cuddling me close.

I probably would have slept all day had it not been for my irritating cell phone ringing. I blindly reach my hand out in the air. Andrew slides out of bed and grasp my purse lying on the floor, he takes out my cell and hands it to me.

"Hello." I say in a raspy voice.

"Jenna, are you still at Andrew's?" Christie asks me.

"Yes."

"When are you coming here?"

"I don't feel that great Christie. I need to sleep a little while longer."

"Okay. Call me when you're on your way." She tells me.

"Okay." I hang up my cell, throwing it on the floor and curl back to the pillow. I sleep for a few hours longer.

My pounding head wakes me, I turn to my side and Andrew is not there. I stand up and slide my jeans on, still wearing his t-shirt I walk out of the bedroom to the living room. Eric and Matt stand as they see me.

"How are you feeling?" Eric asks me.

"Terrible. I can't believe I feel this bad from a few drinks." I tell him.

"Next time drink more." Eric responds, laughing.

I walk over to the couch and sit down. I lay my head on the arm of the couch and curl up in a ball. Andrew walks into the living room, smiling as he sees me curled up on the couch. He snatches a blanket lying across the chair and covers me up. I look up at him, smiling.

"Thank you." He sits next to me.

"You drank more than you realized." He says to me.

"I feel it." I move and lean against him.

"I'm cold." I tell him. He drapes his arm around me and I cuddle close to him.

"You use me for body heat." He says to me jokingly.

"Yep." I respond smiling as I nod.

"You are so greedy." He says jokingly.

"I am! And selfish, too." I respond laughing.

"You sure are."

"Oh shit, I let Matisse out... Watch out!" Eric yells, warning us from the kitchen. A large dog runs through the living room, jumping up on me.

"Down, Matisse!" Andrew says to him. The dog jumps off the couch, sitting on the ground.

"Sorry about that Jenna, he thinks he's a lap dog." Andrew tells me, shaking his head. Matisse looks up at me, slobber runs down his face as his tail shakes. I place my hands on his side, rubbing him.

"You are so cute." I say to him, smiling. He jumps back up on me, knocking me over on the couch.

"Down, Matisse." Andrew says sternly. Matisse jumps down and sits in front of me. I pet him.

"Don't yell at him." I tell Andrew madly. He laughs.

"Most girls don't like big dogs."

"I love all animals." I tell him. "What is he?" I ask him as I continue to pet Matisse.

"A Bull Mastiff. He's six months old."

"You're just a baby." I say to Matisse. I stand up.

"I need the bathroom?" I ask Andrew.

"You can use the one in my bedroom." He responds.

"Can I use your toothbrush?" He nods. I walk into the bathroom and Matisse follows me.

"Come here Matisse." Andrew says to him.

"It's okay, he can come with me." I tell Andrew. He nods and I take Matisse with me into the bathroom.

I brush my teeth and wash my face. I walk to the bedroom, grab my purse, and find a ponytail and a brush. I brush my hair and tie it up on my head. I walk back out to the living room with Matisse in tow.

"Feel better?" Andrew asks me.

"Much better, thank you." I respond to him.

I start to play with Matisse. Andrew watches.

"Can I take him outside?" I ask him.

"Sure."

I walk to the door wall, opening it. Matisse runs out instantly, and I follow. Matisse and I run around the yard. He knocks me down a few times and I begin to wrestle with him, rolling in the grass. Andrew walks outside and joins in wrestling with Matisse and rolling on the grass. Matisse runs back to the house, Eric lets him in and I sit up, Andrew sits next to me.

"I really have to get to my sisters. I need a shower, I smell like a brewery." I say to Andrew with disgust.

"You do smell." He responds jokingly. I push him down. He retaliates and we start play wrestling in the grass.

"Jenna!" I sit up and see Ben madly walking towards me. I stand up quickly as he approaches. I am not prepared for his open hand hitting me. I lose my balance and fall to the ground. Andrew rushes towards him, Rocco restrains him. Bodyguards surround us.

"What the hell are you doing?" Andrew yells angrily. Eric and Matt rush outside. Two of the other bodyguards restrain them. Ben grabs my arm, pulling me forcibly up.

"You whore!" He yells as he stands me up. He hits me again, I plummet to the ground. I feel my eye swell.

"Get your hands off of her!" Andrew screams. Ben hits me again, and I fall to the ground.

"What the fuck man, stop it!" Matt screams.

"You better hope I don't get loose!" Eric screams angrily. Andrew looks up at Rocco.

"How can you watch him do this to her?" Andrew says to Rocco, distraught. Ben picks me up. Rocco walks over to the other bodyguard, handing Andrew to him. As Ben lifts his hand in the air to hit me again, Rocco grabs it.

"That's enough, Senator." Rocco says to him sternly. Ben nods and Rocco releases his hand. He walks over to me, extending his hand to me. I take it.

"Come on Mrs. Kramer." He says to me. I stand and he places his arm around me, comforting me as tears fall down my face.

"Take her to the car." Ben says to Rocco. Rocco nods. I gaze at Andrew, a light smile encompasses his face. Ben walks up to Andrew.

"If I didn't hold your father in such a high regard I would fire you. Stay away from my wife!" Ben tells him sneering.

I sit on the bed, staring at the blank wall as the bloody belt marks that encrust my body sear painfully. My mind wanders to the dark place, the place where only I can go.

For two days I lie listlessly in bed. The lost, empty feeling is more than I can handle. Ben leaves as normal, taking the first flight to New Hampshire for three days. I need relief from this life of hurt and pain. I throw on a tank top and sweats and walk down to the liquor store. I purchase a bottle of Tequila and make my way to the cliff. Night had fallen and the lake was so silent.

The wind blows briskly across my face. I stare down at the sandy beach. Free. I am free. My mind wanders into the dark place, the place where only I can go.

Sadness encompasses me and I lift my heels up, tip-toeing on the edge of the cliff. I wanted to be free, free of all the pain that I had endured from Ben, free from the heartache. I close my eyes and I feel the wind push my body forward. I would put my fate in the hands of nature.

I feel arms wrap around me and I tumble backwards to the ground. I turn to the side of me, and Andrew is lying on the ground. He sits up immediately.

"Are you crazy? You could have been killed!" He says frantically.

I sit up. I see my bottle of Tequila to the side of me. I grab it, taking the cap off. As I place it to my mouth, Andrew abruptly takes it away.

"No more of that." He says as he pours it out on the ground. I stand up and stumble towards the parking lot. Andrew follows me.

"Where are you going?" he asks me.

"Home." I respond sadly. He stops me, and turns me to face him.

"Where is Ben?" Andrew asks me.

"Gone." I respond to him. He places his hand in mine.

"I'm taking you home with me." He says sternly.

He walks me to his car and opens the passenger door. He gently helps me inside then walks over, getting in on the driver's side. He reaches over me, attaching my seat belt.

"What are you doing here?"

"Looking for you."

"Why?" I ask him.

"I was worried about you. It's been two days, I've been calling and texting you. Why didn't you call or text me back?" He asks worriedly.

"I didn't have anything to say."I say as tears fall down my face.

"He hurt you again, didn't he?" He asks with anguish in his eyes.

I nod and start to sob uncontrollably.

"Oh, baby." He says distraught, as he embraces me tightly.

"He will never let us be together." I say with devastation.

"He doesn't have a choice. I'm never letting go. You are coming with me."

"He will never stop coming for me, Andrew."

"I will never let him take you again, I promise. I will always protect you Jenna. You are everything to me. I need you… I need to be with you." He kisses me softly on the lips. I sit back on my seat.

He starts the car and I stare out at the window, going to the dark place, the place where only I can go.

I'm interrupted by Andrew placing his hand on mine. I turn to him.

"Do me favor, don't think so much." He says to me. I smile at him.

Andrew parks and we walk into the house. Eric and Matt are sitting on the couches watching television.

"Your husband is a real asshole." Matt says with disgust.

"I swear if I ever get that guy alone, I'm going to punch his lights out!" Eric chimes in.

"Cut it out, she doesn't need to hear this." We walk up to Eric.

"Sit with Matt, so Jenna and I can sit here." Andrew says to Eric. Eric nods and moves over to the other couch. We sit down.

"Where is Matisse?" I ask aloud.

"We had him neutered. He is staying the night at the veterinarian hospital."

"Why would you do that to him?" I ask Andrew astounded.

"We don't want him going around the neighborhood knocking up the bitches." Matt says, laughing. Andrew and Eric laugh loudly at Matt's comment.

"That was a good one." Eric tells Matt. I sit up.

"You are the ones who need to be neutered!" I say madly. Andrew wraps his arms around me, pulling me close to him.

"They're only joking around, Jenna." I shake my head and sit back.

"What are you guys watching?" Andrew asks them.

"Some mystery movie, I don't know Eric put it on." Matt tells him. I yawn and Andrew turns to me.

"Are you tired?" He asks me. I nod my head. He drapes his arm around me and I lay my head on his shoulder. My eyes become droopy as I watch the movie. Andrew smiles at me.

"Do you want to go to bed?" he asks me. I nod my head. He stands up and extends his hand to me. I take it and we walk into the bedroom.

I walk over to the bed and start to remove my jewelry, placing it on the nightstand. Andrew walks up behind me. He runs his hands gently up and down my arms, sending shivers throughout my body. I turn facing him kissing him with want, with need. His kisses are slow and soft. He removes my shirt, and softly caresses my back as he kisses me. He unclasps my bra, and then slides my sweats and panties off, till I'm standing naked before him.

"You're so beautiful." he says in a whisper. I kiss him urgently, undressing him. He picks me up, laying me gently on the bed. He moves on top of me, just staring in my eyes. I move my hands, clutching his back, pulling him to me. We kiss messy and hard, passionate and lovingly. He lifts his head up, staring amorously into my eyes.

As we make love, I hold him close to me, wanting to remember his strong shoulders, the touch of his skin to mine. He lies on top of me as he regains his strength. I run my hands gently up and down his back. He lifts his head to look in my eyes, kissing me softly.

"I love you Jenna."

"I love you too."

We fall asleep in the warmth of each other's arms. I wake in the middle of the night and call a cab. I kiss Andrew softly on the forehead and leave.

I slide into my bed and fall back to sleep.

I wake in the morning to my phone buzzing. I grasp it from my nightstand.

"Where did you go?" Andrew text.

"I had to leave."

"Why?"

"I don't want Ben coming there."

"I am not afraid of Ben. Come back over."

"Andrew, I don't know."

"Don't think so much, just come over." His text reads. I smile at his text.

"Okay. I'm going to shower then I'll be back over."

"See you soon."

I decide to make dinner for Andrew and his roommates. I stop at the grocery store and pick up all the ingredients needed to make

Veal Parmesan. I drive to Andrew's house. I stumble, carrying the bags. I place my face on the doorbell. Eric answers.

"Let me help you with that." Eric says as he grabs some of the bags. He walks them into the kitchen. Andrew walks in behind us.

"What are you doing?" he asks me. I smile at him.

"I'm going to make dinner for everyone."

"Can I help?" he asks sweetly.

"Do you know how to make Veal Parmesan?" I ask him with a grin.

"No, but you can show me." He tells me. I nod. I take two bowls out and scramble three eggs in one and place bread crumbs in the other.

"Take a Veal patty, place it in the egg, and then the breading." I place a platter next to him. "And then put it on here." I tell him. He nods his head, smiling. I turn on the stove and place tomato paste and water in the pot. I place stewed tomatoes on a cutting board. I gently pound one of the tomatoes and it flies in the air, hitting Andrew in the face. I laugh immediately.

"I'm so sorry. I didn't mean that." I say to him. He takes the kitchen towel and wipes his face.

"Oh you are going to pay for that!" He responds. I back up slowly, placing my hands in front of me.

"Andrew, it was an accident!" I tell him. He throws the kitchen towel on the counter.

"Oh baby, you are in so much trouble!" He states sternly. I run to the door wall and out to the yard.

"Stop Andrew!" I scream as he chases me. He grabs me and we tumble to the ground. I turn to face him as he lies on top of me.

"I didn't mean it." I say to him grinning. He stares into my eyes and lightly brushes the hair from my face. My heart starts to beat fast as he moves his face closer to mine. It wasn't a want or a lust as I looked into his eyes; it was love, simply love.

The door wall opens, catching our attention.

"Something is burning." Matt screams. We both stand and run into the house. Without thinking, I take the red hot pan off the stove, scalding my hand. I throw it in the sink.

"Ow." I scream in pain. Andrew grabs my hand. He turns on the faucet, placing it under cold water. He grabs a kitchen towel and dabs my hand staring at it. He removes the towel and lifts my hand, placing gentle kisses on it. A tingling sensation fills my body.

Eric walks into the room. I pull my hand away.

"I am going to go get my cream from my purse and put it on my hand." I tell Andrew. He nods and I walk away. Eric stands in front of Andrew.

"What are you doing?" Eric says to him worriedly.

"I love her Eric." Andrew responds.

"She's married Andrew."

"I'm aware of that."

"Don't get me wrong, Jenna is amazing, Andrew, but her husband is vicious. You've seen what he did to her, he wouldn't hesitate to do worse to you."

"I know what I'm doing, Eric."

"Do you?" he asks him. Andrew leans against the counter, exhaling, Eric leaves.

After dinner, we all sit around, watching television. I fall asleep on the couch, and Andrew carries me into his room, laying me on the bed. He slides my jeans off and slides in next to me, cuddling me close.

My cell rings in the middle of the night. I grasp it out of my purse.

"Hello." I answer.

"Jenna, Ben is on his way to our house. I told him you were sleeping. You have to get here quick." Christie says to me.

I jump out of bed and dress quickly. Andrew stands up.

"What's wrong?" he asks me sleepily.

"Ben is on his way to Christies." I rush to the front door. Andrew stops me.

"Jenna, I don't want you going back there. Stay here with me."

"I can't do that right now. I need time to work things out."

"I don't want you to go." He says sadly.

"I don't want to go, but I have to." I place my hand on the door knob.

"Wait." Andrew says as he walks up to me. He bends his head, kissing me softly. I smile with my eyes closed as he lifts his head.

"You like that, huh?" I nod my head. He bends his head, kissing me again.

"I'll see you soon." I grab the doorknob and stop suddenly. The thought of leaving Andrew hits me hard. Tears fall down my face. He embraces me tightly.

"Hey." He says softly.

"I'm sorry. I'm such a baby."

"You're not a baby. You don't have to leave, you can stay." He says to me sadly. I embrace him tightly.

"I can't Andrew, not now." At the risk of changing my mind, I run out the door and to my car.

I jump in my car and speedily drive to Christies. Christie opens the door widely as I step out of the car.

"Hurry up, Jenna!" She screams. I run into the house and quickly change into a silk teddy. I slide under the covers. A knock at the door makes me jump. I lie in the bed and listen. Christie answers the door, and I hear Ben talking to her. I turn away from the door and curl to my pillow. The bedroom door opens and Ben walks over to my bed, sitting down. He strokes my head gently.

"Darling." He whispers. I turn with my eyes half opened.

"Hi." I respond to him. I fake stretch and yawn, sitting up.

"I'm taking you home." He says to me. He stands up and grasps my suitcase and takes out a dress. He walks back over to the bed and slides it over my head. He scoops me in his arms and carries me out of the house to the limo. He lays me gently inside the limo, and slides in next to me. He wraps his arm around me, cuddling me close.

I wake in the morning and shower. After I dress I walk out to the patio with a cup of coffee. I sit down and stare out to the clear blue sky, thinking of Andrew.

"Good morning, darling." Ben says as he walks out to the patio, he bends, kissing me on the cheek and sits down next to me. He drinks his coffee as he reads his newspaper. I gaze at him and he looks different, like a stranger, someone I no longer knew. I stand up. He grasps my hand.

"Where are you going?" he asks me nicely.

"Inside." I respond simply. He nods his head. I walk into the house and turn on the morning news. Again, Ben is the top story.

"Things are getting really heated up with New Hampshire Senator Hillary Barker and Senator Benjamin Kramer. We caught up with the Senators when they were having a romantic dinner at The Chian"…"

A picture flashes of Ben and Hillary locked in a passionate kiss. Embarrassed and angry, I shake my head as I look down.

"Jenna." Ben says to me. I turn to him and he stares at me, distraught. I rush down the hall to the bedroom and grasp my suitcase, he follows me.

"What are you doing?" he asks me.

"I'm leaving you." I respond to him. He grabs my arms.

"Jenna, I'm sorry." He says to me. I start hitting him wildly.

"How could you do this to me!" I scream madly. He embraces me tightly.

"I'm sorry. I'm so sorry." He says emotionally. I push him away and open the dresser drawers, dumping my clothes in the suitcase.

"She can have you, because I don't want you anymore!" I say to him disconcerted. I grasp my suitcase and walk out the back door. He follows me.

"Please, Jenna, it won't happen again!" He pleads. I stop and turn to him.

"I'm done with you!" I grasp my suitcase, throw it into the car, and drive to Christies.

Christie had also watched the news, so I wasn't surprised that she was waiting on the porch when I drove up. She was surprised when she didn't see a tear on my face.

"You're not upset about Ben's affair?"

"No. Not at all. I really want to be with Andrew, Christie." I say to her sadly. She embraces me.

"I know."

Christie and Manny watch movies as I lay on the couch watching with them. I fall asleep and Manny covers me up with a blanket.

I am awoken by the pounding of the door. Manny walks over to it opening it. Ben rushes in. Manny places his hand on his chest pushing him back.

"Get out. You are not welcomed in my home." Manny tells him angrily.

"I came to get my wife!" Ben says to him madly. Rocco walks in, restraining Manny.

"Get the fuck out of my house now!" Manny screams. Christie walks over to the couch, embracing me tightly. Ben walks over to us. He extends his hand to me.

"Let's go, darling, it's time to go home." Ben says to me. A body guard walks over to the couch, restraining Christie.

"Get you fucking hands off of my wife!" Manny screams. Ben grabs my hand and I pull away from him.

"I'm not going anywhere with you!" I say to him madly. I felt only hate for him. All the abuse, the cheating, I had had enough.

"You are my wife, you belong with me!" He grabs my elbows pulling me up. I spit in his face and he releases me.

"I don't belong with you. You belong with Hillary!" I tell him angrily. He wipes the spit from his face, then without warning, he raises his hand, hitting me across the face. I fall to the ground.

"You son of a bitch!" Manny screams loudly. Ben extends his hand to me.

"Let's go, darling." He says calmly.

"I'm not going anywhere with you Ben!" I tell him again.

He scoops me into his arms and carries me out of the house. He places me in the limo. I hit him, and he back hands me across the face. I clench my fist and start punching him. I crawl on top of him, hitting him over and over again.

"I hate you! I hate you!" I scream. The limo pulls into the driveway. The door opens and Rocco pulls me off of Ben, smiling. Ben sits up, his hair is messy and his lip is bleeding. He walks towards me and I start kicking.

"I hate you! Stay away from me!" I scream madly. Ben looks at me astounded and backs away.

"Please take Mrs. Kramer inside." Ben tells Rocco, his voice shaking. Rocco walks me into the bedroom, setting me on the bed. He leaves closing the door.

Chapter VI

Infuriated and aggravated, I sit impatiently on the bed as I tap my foot on the floor. Ben walks into the room, and a look of disgust encompasses my face instantly. He is carrying papers in his hand, he throws them at me. I glance at them, and they are all the text messages between Andrew and me. I look up at him.

"So, you are sleeping with Andrew?" He says madly.

"So, You have been sleeping with women are whole marriage." I retort. He walks closer to me and places his hand on his belt.

"You are not to see him ever again! Do you hear me!" he screams loudly.

"I love him and I am going to be with him." I retort. He raises his hand, smacking me hard across the face.

"You are mine Jenna. Forever… forever…" He says to me, his voice hoarsely frightening.

"No. I am not yours!" I attempt to run towards the bedroom door, but he grabs me. I fight him off and we fall to the ground. I crawl on the ground, desperately attempting to flee Ben.

"You think you can get away from me?" He screams like a maniac, then lifts his foot and slams it down on my arm. I scream as I feel the bones crack. He loses complete control as he lets the anger fill him deeper. He slams his foot down over and over, until my arm is so broken, it's numb.

"Lie on the bed now!" he screams to me.

I crawl, with my good arm dragging my broken arm, and lift myself slowly onto the bed. I lie on my stomach, awaiting my punishment.

His infuriation is so deep. He slides the gold buckle dark brown leather belt out of the loops of his pants and starts hitting me across my legs and lower back, like a crazed lunatic. I lay helplessly on the bed, taking the punishment. He doesn't tire easily and I can feel every part of my body burning as the bloody belt marks sear through me.

When he's finished he leaves the bedroom. I stare at the blank wall. A deep depression overwhelms me, and my want to die grows stronger as the throbbing through my body is unbearable. I attempt to lift myself up, but the marks send stabbing pains through my muscles, weakening me. I fall back on the bed and sob. I attempt to go to the dark place, but the pain that encompassed my body overshadows my mind.

Ben walks back into the room.

"You are mine Jenna, forever… forever, only mine!" he says in a frightening tone. I nod my head, tears falling down my face.

I lay, awaiting the soothing cream. But Ben has more in store for me. I feel the deep scalding of my skin as he presses something down on it. I scream as the pain scorches through me, and the smell of my own burning skin fills my senses. The agonizing pain hovers, even after he removes the branding tool.

"You're mine… forever… forever." he says frighteningly quiet. My head clouds as the dizziness fills it, I close my eyes and wither off into a slumber.

I wake in the morning and my body aches with agony. I cannot feel my right arm. I lie on my stomach, unable to move. Ben is gone and I am alone to deal with the pain and suffering that not only encompassed my body, but also encompassed my soul.

My cell rings and I am unable to move my arm to retrieve it. My mind wanders to the dark place, the place where only I can go.

For hours I lay still, staring at the blank wall. The bedroom door opens and Andrew rushes into the room. He looks down at my naked, broken body horrified. He sits on the bed next to me and raises a sheet, covering me up. Eric and Matt walk into the room.

"Call an ambulance, she's hurt bad!" Andrew tells Eric with devastation. I cannot lift my head or move, so Andrew lies on the bed, staring into my eyes.

"I'm here. I'm not going to leave you, I promise." He says to me. I can see the hurt and pain in his eyes.

The ambulance arrives, and two men lift me from the bed and gently place me on my stomach on the gurney. Andrew holds my hand as they walk me out to the ambulance. Ben walks up as they roll me to the back of the ambulance. Rocco sees me on the gurney and turns, walking back to the limo. He steps inside of it, leaving Ben alone.

"What's going on here? Where are you going with my wife?" Ben says, acting confused. Andrew rushes up to him, Eric and Matt stand in between Ben and Andrew.

"You beat her? And left her to suffer!" Andrew screams angrily.

"I don't know what you're talking about. What are you doing here anyways?" Ben asks him angrily. Eric turns to Andrew.

"Go with Jenna. We will take care of him. She needs you right now." Eric says calmly to Andrew. He nods and turns and rushes to the back of the ambulance, stepping inside. Ben lunges forward, and Eric pushes him back.

"Stay right there, Senator, and no one will get hurt." Eric says with a smirk.

"Rocco. Get these guys out of my face!" Ben says aloud. Rocco doesn't come, he looks around, and sees Rocco is nowhere in sight. He exhales.

Andrew holds my hand, and with his other hand, he strokes my head gently.

The doctor examines me as Andrew waits out in the waiting room, pacing nervously. He had called Christie and Manny. They rush into the emergency room, running up to Andrew.

"What's going on?" Manny asks him.

"She's with the doctor right now." Andrew responds, devastated.

"What's wrong with her?" Christie asks Andrew. They walk into the waiting room, sitting down.

"He beat her again, he broke her arm…" He says, tearfully overwhelmed with grief. Christie rubs his back.

"It's okay Andrew." She says, softly attempting to comfort him. He lifts his head, squeezing his eyes closed tightly as he attempts to choke out the words.

"He branded her." He chokes out. Manny stands astounded by Andrew's words.

"What?"

"He burned the words "MINE" into her lower back, and then he left her to suffer all by herself." Andrew continues, distraught. Manny paces; enraged, confused, and hurt. He rushes back over to Andrew and embraces him.

"It's okay Andrew. We will get through this together." Manny tells him. Andrew nods.

Patiently, they wait for two hours. Andrew calls his parents and explains what is going on. They immediately schedule a flight from New York to Michigan.

The doctor walks into the emergency room.

"Jenna Kramer!" He yells. Andrew runs up, followed by Christie and Manny.

"We're here for Jenna." Andrew tells him. He places his arm around Andrew, and they all walk over to a corner in the waiting room, sitting down.

"I am Dr. Lewis. Jenna just got out of surgery. Jenna's arm has some pretty bad breaks. It has a distal radius fracture, and an ulna fracture; both required plates and screws to stabilize the bones. She also has a radial head fracture, which required pins and screws to repair it, the surgeries all went well. We put her on a medicated cream for her wounds on her back." The doctor explains to us.

"So she is good?" Andrew says with excitement.

"She is stable, but she doesn't seem to want to wake up."

"She was awake when she was in an ambulance." Andrew says, distraught.

"I know. It happened right before surgery. We have attempted many times to wake her, but she's non-responsive."

"Can we see her?" Andrew asks the doctor. The doctor nods and stands.

"Follow me." The doctor tells them. They follow the doctor down the hall to the Intensive Care Unit. As the doctor reaches the room, he turns to them.

"We had to put her on a ventilator, so she is not breathing on her own." The doctor tells them.

Andrew stands by the door, staring at me, he gasps as he sees the machines around me. He quietly walks over to my bed and places his hand in mine. He bends his head, kissing my hand, and then places his head on the bed, sobbing. Christie rushes into the room, embracing him.

"It's okay Andrew, she is going to be okay, I promise." Christie says to him. Manny walks in and wraps his arms around both of them.

Andrew sat for four days next to my bed, never leaving. I begin to breathe on my own, and the nurse removes the ventilator. They are still unable to wake me. I am in the dark place, the place where only I can go.

As the nurse shuts out the lights, Andrew stands over me.

"I promise I will never let him hurt you again. Wherever you are, Jenna, please come back to me. I need you… I love you… I love you." He kisses me on the forehead and sits back down on the chair.

I choke as I take in a deep breath. Andrew leans over me.

"Jenna." He says with desperation. I move my head back and forth. I attempt to open my eyes, but my heavy lids refute me. I attempt again, and slowly they open. The bright light burns, I squeeze my eyes tightly. Finally after a few backward rolls they open. I stare up at Andrew, smiling.

"Hi." I say groggily.

"Hi." He says softly. Tears fall down his face. I lift my hand and wipe his tears.

"I missed you, Jenna." He says tearfully. He embraces me tightly.

"I missed you too." I respond to him.

"I love you." He says sniffling.

"I love you too."

Christie and Manny walk into the room, and they rush up to me. Andrew steps aside.

"Jenna!" Christie says, sobbing. She embraces me tightly. "I thought I was going to lose you."

"I'm here." I tell her. She lifts her head and nods. Manny embraces me.

"Oh kid. You are going to be the death of me!" Manny says tearfully.

"I love you, Manny."

"I love you too, Jenna." He responds as he holds me tight.

"Do you remember what happened?" Manny asks me.

"Yes." I respond. He exhales.

The doctor walks in and checks my eyes and reflexes. He checks my arm, and the wounds on my back, then leaves. Andrew sits on the chair next to me, holding my hand.

"How are you feeling?" he asks me.

"Sore." I tell him.

The nurse walks into the room, pushing a wheel chair. The beating had left me weak, my back was so sore it weakened my legs, so the doctor didn't want me walking until I healed. The nurse lifts the blanket off of me, and Andrew stares at my casted arm, shaking his head. The nurse walks over to me.

"Place your good arm around my neck and I'll help you up." The nurse instructs me. Andrew walks up, scoops me into his arms, and gently places me in the wheel chair. The nurse giggles.

"Or he can just pick you up." She says with a smile.

"Sorry." Andrew responds, blushing.

"Oh, it's fine." The nurse tells him. She pushes me into the bathroom, closing the door. She wheels my wheelchair to the toilet.

"Now grab the rail with your good arm and pick yourself off of the wheelchair and on to the toilet." She instructs. I place my hand on the rail and attempt to lift myself to the toilet, but am unsuccessful. My good arm is too weak to lift my body, and I tumble to the ground, hitting the wheel chair with my leg, sending it flying into the wall, causing a loud crashing noise. The bathroom door opens abruptly, and Andrew rushes into the room. He sees me lying on the ground and scoops me up into his arms.

"What are you doing to her?" Andrew asks the nurse madly.

"It wasn't her fault. My arm is too weak I couldn't lift myself up." I tell him.

"I got her." Andrew tells the nurse. She nods her head and leaves, closing the door. Andrew places me on the toilet and stares at me. "Are you going to go or not?" Andrew asks me impatiently.

"I can't go in front of you, Andrew." I tell him, embarrassed.

He exhales.

"Ok. I will be right outside the door, just yell for me when you're finished. Promise me you will not attempt to get off of there by yourself." He says to me with seriousness.

"I promise." I tell him. He nods his head and leaves. I finish using the bathroom and flush the toilet.

"Andrew!" I yell. He opens the door and smiles as he scoops me into his arms. He carries me back to the bed, lying me down gently, covering me up

"You need anything else?" he asks me pleasantly. I shake my head.

"Thank you." He places his hand in mine.

"I didn't know attorneys made hospital calls." Ben says sarcastically as he walks into the room. Andrew stands, and anger fills him. He lunges towards Ben, but Manny stops him.

"If I were you Ben, I would leave." Manny says with a sneer to him.

"I came to see my wife." Ben responds calmly. He walks towards my bed.

Andrew places his hand on Ben's shoulder, lightly pushing him back.

"That's far enough." Andrew says to him sternly. Ben chuckles.

"Isn't there some privacy clause in an attorney/client contract that states that you're not allowed to sleep with their wife?" Ben asks Andrew rudely. Andrew lets out a sarcastic chuckle and walks closer to Ben.

"If you were taking care of your wife, then I wouldn't have had to." Andrews comment infuriates Ben.

Ben attempts to hit Andrew, but Andrew blocks it then raises his clenched fist and hits Ben in the face, knocking him to the ground. Manny laughs as he rushes over to Andrew's side. Ben stands and retrieves a handkerchief from his pocket, wiping his mouth.

"You're going to regret that!" Ben says as he wipes the blood from his lip.

"The only regret I have is ever letting her go back to you. I can assure you it will never happen again."

"She belongs to me. She is mine, not even you can change that."

Andrew lunges at him, and Manny restrains him.

"Just leave Ben." Manny tells him. Ben chuckles and turns around, walking away.

Manny turns to Andrew as he grunts. "Calm down, tiger." Manny says jokingly. Andrew walks back over to my bed, sitting down. He places his hand in mine.

"I will never let him hurt you again." I smile at his comment. Christie and Manny walk over to the opposite side of my bed.

"So, are you finally going to divorce him?" Christie asks me.

"Yes." I respond to her.

"Good. I will be happy to be rid of that pedophile woman beater." Manny says to me sternly.

"You can stay with us as long as you want, Jenna." Christie offers.

"Thank you." She embraces me tightly.

"I love you, Jenna."

"I love you too."

Christie and Manny leave after a few hours. Andrew stays.

"You don't have to stay. I will be okay by myself." I tell him.

"No way. I'm not leaving you." He says to me sweetly. I scoot over on my bed, patting the side next to me. Andrew slides in next to me and wraps his arms around me, cuddling me close.

I wake to something squeezing my arm. I open my eyes and see a blood pressure cuff attached to my arm. I stare up at the nurse. She places her finger over her mouth then points to my side. I turn and Andrew is sleeping soundly. I nod, smiling at her. She finishes taking my vitals and leaves. I move closer to Andrew and he wraps his arms around me, cuddling me close.

"Hello." I open my eyes; William and Wendy walk in. Andrew stands up and kisses his mothers cheek.

"Hi mother." Andrew says to her.

"Hi son, how are you doing?" she asks him worriedly.

"I'm okay." He responds. He shakes his father's hand.

"How are you holding up, son?" William asks him.

"I'm okay." He responds. Wendy walks over to me smiling; she places her hands on my cheek.

"So pretty." She says sweetly. She kisses my cheek. William walks over, kissing my cheek.

"How are you feeling, Jenna?" William asks me.

"I'm sore." I tell him with a smile.

"Knock, knock." Detective Mason says as he walks into the room.

"Hi." I say to me. I attempt to lift myself up, but am unsuccessful as my weakened muscles do not cooperate. Andrew walks over to me and gently pulls me up, he forgets about the wounds on my back, and pulls too hard. I scream as the pain sears through me.

"Ow!" Andrew looks at me, devastated.

"Sorry Jenna." He says sorrowfully. The nurse hears my scream and walks into the room.

"What happened?" the nurse asks me.

"I tried to move her up, and I think I hit her back." Andrew says to the nurse, disconcerted.

"Let me check." The nurse says to Andrew. He steps out of the way and she turns me over. She undoes the ties on the back of my gown and then stares at the bloody belt marks. Detective Mason looks at my wounds, mortified.

"Dear God." He says aloud. William walks over to Andrew.

"Ben did that to her?" he asks horrified.

"Yes."

Tears fill Wendy's eyes. William wraps his arms around her, comforting her.

The nurse places cream on my wounds, and then turns me back over.

"I will wrap it later. The doctor wants it to get air right now, so it will scab up." The nurse explains to me. I nod my head and the nurse leaves. Detective Mason walks up to me.

"Are you ready to give a statement?" Detective Mason asks me. I nod my head. He opens his briefcase and retrieves a yellow legal pad and a pen. "Ok Jenna, tell me what happened."

"I found out about Ben's affair with Senator Barker and left him. I went to my sisters and he came over there, and forcibly took me back home. We got into a physical altercation, in the limo and I hit him over and over. One of his bodyguards pulled me off of him when we arrived at the house. He took me into the bedroom, placing me on the bed. Ben came in and he placed his hand on his belt like he was going to beat me. I told him no and tried to leave the bedroom but he stopped me. I tried to fight him off, and we ended up in a wrestling match. I fell on the ground and attempted to leave the room crawling on the ground, it's when he slammed his foot on my arm, he did it over and over, for about fifteen minutes, I felt my arm go numb. He then ordered me to lie on the bed, for my usual punishment." I explain to him.

"Usual punishment?" Detective Mason asks, confused.

"Yes. Whenever Ben was angry he would punish me with his belt." I tell Detective Mason. He looks down, shaking his head.

"Continue please." Detective Mason says softly.

"He hit me for awhile with the belt, and then left the room. Normally, he would come back in the room and rub a cream on my back, so I laid there waiting, when I felt the burning. I could feel my skin melting, I could smell it, and it was an indescribable, agonizing pain that lingered even after he took the branding tool off my back." I continue.

William leans over to Andrew's ear.

"He's branded her?" William asks Andrew with disbelief.

"Yes." Andrew responds as tears fill his eyes. William wraps his arm around him, comforting him.

"When did the beating occur?" Detective Mason asks me.

"About 3 a.m." I answer. He looks down at the hospital paper work.

"Wait, you didn't get to the hospital until after 11:00 a.m. He left you for eight hours by yourself after he beat you so badly?" Detective Mason asks me astounded.

"Yes. He does it every time he beats me. It is his way of making me suffer and think about why I was punished." I answer. Detective Mason shakes his head. He walks over to the door and unclips his walkie-talkie from his pants pocket.

"I want Senator Benjamin Kramer picked up." He says simply.

"Okay." An officer answers.

"I will be down at the station within fifteen minutes." Detective Mason continues. He clips his walkie-talkie back on his pants pocket and walks back over to me.

"Jenna, I am going to pick your husband up for domestic violence. In a domestic violence case there is an automatic no contact order issued, so Benjamin Kramer will not be able to contact you." He explains he reaches into his pocket and hands me his card.

"If he contacts you, you call me." Detective Mason says to me sternly. I nod my head.

"Thank you." I respond to him. He smiles and then turns and leaves. Andrew walks over and sits on the chair next to my bed.

"Andrew, you're his attorney, don't you have to help him?" I ask him worriedly. William walks over to my bed.

"When he did this to you, he stopped being our client. I can assure you he will not be calling us." William tells me. I smile, nodding my head. Wendy walks up to the bed, standing next to William.

"We are going to go, Jenna. We will be back tomorrow to visit." Wendy says sweetly. Andrew moves away from the bed and Wendy hugs me.

"Thank you for coming." I tell her.

"When you get better, I want you to come to New York and see me." She responds with a smile. I nod my head. William bends kissing me on the cheek.

"Rest and get better." He says to me. Andrew shakes his father's hand and hugs his mother and they leave. He sits back down on the chair next to my bed.

"You don't have to stay, Andrew. I'm sure you have a lot of work to do." I tell him.

"I am the boss remember, they will be fine without me. I'm staying with you." He explains to me.

"Okay."

Andrew was quite useful in carrying me back and forth to the bathroom. As he carries me back from a bathroom trip. He stops before reaching the bed.

"Let's go out of this room for awhile." He says to me. He carries me out of the room and down to a waiting room on the floor. He sits me down on a couch near the window. I stare out and can see the lake, I smile.

"Did you know it was here?" I ask him.

"Yes. It's why I brought you in here. I knew you would love the view." He tells me. I turn and face him, smiling.

"Thank you for being here for me." I tell him with endearing eyes.

"You're my girl. I will always be here for you." His comment brings a big smile to my face.

"How did you know that I was hurt? What made you come to my house?" He exhales.

"I called and texted you and when you didn't answer me. I had this really weird uncomfortable pain in my stomach. I don't know it was strange. I just knew something was wrong." He explains distraught. I place my hand in his.

"I am so glad I have you."

"I am glad to have you also." He responds sweetly.

We go back to the room. After an hour, Eric walks into the room, interrupting our card game of Rummy. He places a bag next to Andrew.

"Here is your stuff." Eric says to Andrew. He walks over to me and kisses me on the cheek.

"How are you feeling, Jenna?" he asks me sweetly.

"I'm okay. Thanks for coming." I respond to him.

"Of course, you are our friend." Eric tells him. Matt rushes in the room, struggling with a very large suitcase, he slams it on the ground.

"Jesus, Andrew, you need to have less clothes!" Matt tells him. Andrew looks at him strangely.

"I said a few things Matt." Andrew says to him.

"I didn't know what a few meant, so I packed the first two drawers of your dresser." Matt responds. Andrew shakes his head.

"Jenna, I am going to have these guys sit with you while I shower, is that okay?" he asks me.

"Sure." I tell him. Eric sits on my bed and Andrew glares at him.

When Andrew walks out of the shower Eric and I are laughing and having a great time. Andrew walks over to us.

"You can go now. I'm finished." He says to Eric.

"I will when I'm done talking to Jenna." Eric responds to him. Andrew walks over, sitting on the chair next to Matt.

"So Jenna, are you getting a divorce?" Eric asks me.

"Yes." I respond to him.

"Well maybe you will let me take you out, when you are single?" he asks me. Andrew stands immediately.

He walks over to the bed and lifts Eric forcibly off of it, walking him to the door.

"She is my girl, Eric." Andrew says to him madly. Eric is shocked instantly as Andrew's aggressive reaction scares him. Matt stands up and walks over to Eric.

"Bye, Jenna." Matt says to me.

"See ya guys."

"I'll see you soon, Jenna." Eric says to me. Andrew glares at him and they leave. Andrew walks back over to my bed, sitting on the chair in front of it.

"I don't like Eric flirting with you." Andrew says, pouting with his arms crossed.

"Are you pouting?" I ask him with chuckle.

"You're my girl." he says, still pouting. I chuckle. I place my hand gently on his face.

"I am your girl." I tell him. He exhales with relief. He stands up.

"Scoot over." He says to me. I slide over and he lies next to me. He retrieves the remote and turns on the television. The nurse walks into the room.

"It's time to shower." She says to me pleasantly. Andrew stands up.

"You are not giving her a shower. The last time you took her to the bathroom you nearly broke her neck!" Andrew says to her worriedly.

"She needs a shower, sir." The nurse says to him.

"I will give her a shower." He tells her. He turns to me. "Do you mind?" Andrew asks me.

"I don't mind. It's not like you haven't seen me naked before." I say to him with a raised eyebrow.

"I definitely don't have a problem staring at your naked body." He says with a smirk.

"Okay. If you need me, call." The nurse tells us. I nod my head and she leaves. Andrew scoops me out of the bed, and carries me to the shower. He places me on the chair, and takes the removable shower head in his hand. He places it on the ground and turns the shower on. He turns to me.

"Now what?" he asks me.

"You have to undo the ties on the back of this gown. I can't do it." I tell him. He nods his head. He slowly unties the ties to my gown, and then stands back in front of me. I chuckle.

"Take the gown off." I tell him. He nods. He places his hands on the gown and slowly removes it. He stares at my naked body.

"You are so beautiful." He says with endearing eyes. I chuckle at him.

"Shower?" I ask him as he continues to stare at me. He nods his head, and picks up the shower head. "If you wet my hair and place some shampoo on it. I think I can wash my own hair." I explain to him. He nods his head. I close my eyes and smile as he places the shower head over my head, and the warm water relaxes me. He squeezes shampoo onto my hair, and I slowly wash it with one hand, he stares at me, still holding the shower head in his hand. I look up at him.

"Can you rinse my hair? I'm getting shampoo in my eyes." I tell him. He places the shower head above my head, and uses his free hand to help the water remove the shampoo.

"Your hair is so soft." He says aloud. He places body wash on a washcloth and I wash my body then he rinses it. He wraps me in a towel then turns the shower off. He picks me up and carries me to the bed, laying me down. He walks to the hospital room door, closing and locking it. He retrieves a gown the nurse left and slides it on me, tying the back of it.

"Thank you. Can you brush my hair? I can't do it with one hand. My brush is in that bag, Christie brought." I say to him, pointing to a bag in the corner. He rummages through the bag and walks back over to the bed, I turn my head, and he lightly runs the brush through my hair. I close my eyes as the brush slides effortlessly down my scalp.

"That feels so good." I say to Andrew. He finishes and places the brush on the table. He lies next to me on the bed. The shower has exhausted me, I lay my head on his shoulder and he drapes his arm around me. I fall fast asleep.

"Wake up sleepy head; you have been sleeping for hours." I open my eyes, and Christie is sitting next to my bed. I turn and Andrew is gone.

"Where's Andrew?" I ask her in a panic. My hearts starts to beat quickly, and I can feel my breathing become sparse.

"Jenna, calm down, he just went to the cafeteria. He will be right back." Christie says to me worriedly. I can't catch my breath and I can't sit up quick enough. My oxygen level decreases quickly and an alarm rings. Nurses rush into my room, and Christie stands by helplessly watching. They place a mask on my face.

"Breathe, Jenna." The nurse says to me. The doctors rush into the room, and everything fades to black.

I feel a hand gently stroking my head, I open my eyes and Andrew is leaning over me. He smiles at me and I smile back. I sit up and take the oxygen mask off.

"I don't think you are supposed to take that off." Andrew says to me as he sits on the bed.

"I'm fine." I tell him.

"What happened, Jenna?" he asks me.

"I don't know. I didn't see you and I panicked. I think I'm really screwed up from what Ben did to me." I respond to him honestly.

"It's understandable." He says as he places his hand in mine.

"You scared the shit out of me." Christie says as she walks over to the side of my bed.

"I'm sorry." I tell her.

"You are definitely going to need some counseling after this." Manny says as he stands next to Christie.

"I know."

"Jenna, my parents invited you for a visit to New York. I talked to the doctor, and he said you should be going home in a few days, so maybe we could go for the weekend. I was talking to Manny and Christie, and we think it would be a good idea for you to get away for awhile." He says to me. I smile at him.

"That's sounds good to me." I tell him.

"Okay. I'll make the arrangements." He says happily.

Christie and Manny visit for awhile and then leave. Andrew and I lie on the bed and watch television.

"Can I ask you something?"

"Of course, you can ask me anything."

"Before me, were you ever in love?"

"No. I didn't know what love was until I met you." He responds amorously.

"I believe your heart can only belong to one person at time. Because, when I fell in love with you, I instantly fell out of love with Ben." I tell him.

"When?" he asks me confused.

"Remember when I came to your office and I was depressed?"

"Yeah."

"It was then. I didn't know that, of course, until now." He smiles, stroking my cheek gently.

"Remember when my father took me out to the hall?"

"Yeah."

"He knew something was going on between you and I. He wiped your lipstick from my mouth with his finger."

"You never told me that."

"I know I never told you. He told me to stop whatever I was doing with you. When I walked back into the office, I was really trying to convince myself that it was wrong and I needed to stop. But I couldn't. The more I was with you, the more I didn't want to be without you." He says emotionally. I place my lips to his, kissing him softly.

"I have to check your vitals." The nurse says, interrupting us. Andrew stands immediately, he walks towards the door.

"Andrew." I blurt out. My heart starts to beat rapidly, and my breathing becomes sparse. Andrew rushes over to me.

"Hey. I'm right here." He says as he strokes my head. "Breathe, Jenna." He continues. I close my eyes and take a deep breath. I open my eyes and begin to sob. All that Ben had did to me surfaced in my tears. The beatings flash through my mind all at once. Andrew embraces me tightly.

"Let it out, baby." He says as he holds me close. I sob and sob until I can't sob anymore. Andrew lays me flat on the bed, and then lies next to me facing me. He strokes my head gently. I smile at him.

"You are my best friend." I tell him. He smiles.

"You are my best friend too." He says to me.

I was happy when they took my arm cast off and put a long arm splint on it and released me from the hospital.

Christie and Manny drive me to the house as Andrew followed in his car. I was still dizzy from the pain medications they had given me at the hospital. I struggle as I walk up the steps at Christies. Andrew rushes up behind us and scoops me into his arms.

"You're taking too long." He says with a smile.

Ben took a plea to avoid prosecution and media attention. By the time he exhausted all of his influences in the court system, he received a slap on the hand and a thousand dollar fine.

Ben called, texted, and emailed me over ten times a day. I would never read what he sent. I would delete it all immediately. My cell rings and the number is unknown. I answer it.

"Hello."

"Hi darling."

"Ben. I don't want to talk to you."

"You are my wife. Why wouldn't you want to talk to me?"

"I am getting divorce. I'm not going to be your wife anymore." He chuckles.

"I will never give you a divorce. You are mine forever… forever." I hang up the phone. He calls back and I remove the battery from my phone, placing it on the nightstand. I lie on the bed and stare at the blank wall.

I wake in the morning at Christies. I sit up and stare out the window. My life with Ben flashes before my eyes, I lie back on the bed, and my mind wanders to the dark place, the place where only I can go.

The bedroom door opens and Andrew walks in. I stare at the blank wall. He walks over to the bed and sits in front of me. He bends, kissing me softly. I smile at him.

"I know now how to get you back to me now." He says with a smirk. He places his hand in mine. He stares down at my fingers as he plays with them.

"We have to get you packed; we're leaving in a few hours for New York."

"What about your parents? Did you tell them about us?" I ask him. He shakes his head.

"No. My parents aren't going to be that happy about this."

"Maybe we shouldn't jump into it." I say to him nervously.

"I love you Jenna. It doesn't matter how my parents feel, all that matters is how you feel and I feel, okay." He says to me slowly.

"Okay." He stands up and packs my suitcase.

A limo drives Andrew and I to the airport to catch our flight to New York. The airport is crowded. Andrew holds my hand tightly as we walk through the gate. We sit only a few minutes, when they call us onto the plane. Andrew and I briskly walk down the corridor, into the plane, and to our seats.

The plane starts to roar as the pilots turn on the engines, my breathing starts to quicken. I close my eyes, grasping tightly to the armrests. Andrew stares at me.

"What's wrong?" Andrew asks me with concern. I swallow hard as my breathing is sparse.

"I don't like flying." I tell him frightened.

The plane starts to taxi down the runway. Andrew reaches over me, attempting to latch my seatbelt. Before he is able to latch it the plane shakes and I spring forward landing in his lap. I wrap my hands around his neck tightly, my cheek pressed next to his. He smirks as he holds me close.

"It's okay, Jenna." he tells me.

"I am so afraid of flying." I say to him.

"I got you. I won't let you go." he says with reassurance. The flight seemed like forever, I fall asleep in Andrew's arms. He brushes the hair from my forehead, waking me.

"We're here." he says softly. I stand up and he takes my hand in is and we leave the plane. His father is smiling as we walk out. Andrew hugs him.

"Ah, you're here." his father says to him. He hugs me.

"Hi Jenna, we're so happy you were able to come." his father says to me.

"I'm happy to be here." I tell him. We follow his father out to the front of the airport where a limo waits. We slide into the limo and drive out of the airport. We drive into New York City and I smile as the city is already decorated for Christmas and its only November. Lights light up throughout the city, the Christmas colors shining brightly. I grin from ear to ear. Andrew leans over me.

"It's very amazing, isn't it?" Andrew asks me.

"Yes. It's beautiful. I have never seen anything so beautiful." I tell him. He smiles at my childlike grin.

We pull up on the side of the road, to an enormous building. The limo driver steps out opening the door. I step out and stare at the large 1900's era décor. Andrew stands beside me.

"Someone lives here? It looks like a hotel." I tell him.

"Yes. This is what I call home." he responds. He takes my hand, and we walk up to the door. The door opens, and a man dressed in a black suit and tie smiles at us.

"Andrew." he says happily.

"Kenton." Andrew responds. He turns to me. "Kenton, this is Jenna Kramer." he introduces. He extends his hand and I take it, shaking it.

"It's very nice to meet you Ms. Kramer." Kenton says to me.

"It's nice to meet you." I respond. He moves to the side and we walk in. The house is immaculate. The floors are of a white Italian marble, and dark cherry wood rails encompass the endless spiral staircase. We walk into the open family room. Antique cherry wood chairs, and couches, upholstered in a floral décor, sit around a large stone fireplace. Andrew walks to a couch, sitting down, and I sit next to him.

Chapter VII

Andrew holds my hand, lightly rubbing it, staring at me, smiling. He releases it as his mother glides effortlessly into the room. Her hair is neatly place atop her head. She is wearing a baby blue jacket and a skirt with a white ruffled top. Andrew stands and walks over to her, kissing her gently on the cheek, placing his hand on her shoulder.

"Hi mother." he says to her. She pats his hand.

"Andrew." she responds happily. He walks back over to the couch, sitting next to me, as she sits down on one of the antique chairs. She smiles as she looks at me.

"Hi Jenna, how are you feeling?" she asks.

"I'm feeling okay, thank you for asking."

Andrew's father walks into the house. He walks up to Andrew's mother, kissing her on the cheek.

"Darling." He says as he places his hand on her shoulder.

We visit for awhile with his parents, and then walk off to the den to relax and watch a movie.

The day was long and I soon fall asleep, resting my head on Andrew's lap, he sits, silently stroking my head as he gazes at me. Andrew's mother walks into the den sitting across from us.

"She's very tired." Andrew's mother says softly.

"Yeah. She's exhausted." He responds to her.

"Andrew, Ben Kramer is telling everyone you stole his wife." Wendy says to Andrew worriedly.

"That is a blatant lie, he lost her because of the way he treated her!" He tells Wendy. She smiles at him.

"You two seem very comfortable together."

"She is great. I love being with her."

"Mhm." His mother states immediately. Andrew looks at her strangely.

"What?" he asks her.

"Nothing son. Nothing at all." She says with a big grin.

"Mother. What is it?" he asks her suspiciously.

"I think you really care about this girl."

"Of course I care about her, she's my best friend."

"Mhm." He rolls his eyes.

"Just spit it out mother." He tells her impatiently.

"All I have to say is that I really want you to be careful son. She comes with a lot of emotional baggage. I don't want to see you get hurt." She says to him worriedly.

"I'm fine mother. I assure you I have no plans of getting hurt."

She nods her head and stands. "Well I have to meet with my friend, Penny. I will see you two later?" she asks as she stands.

"Of course." She walks to the door.

The closing of the door wakes me. I sit up, stretching. I smile at Andrew.

"Sorry, I fell asleep." I tell him.

"It's fine." He responds.

"So are you going to show me Central Park?" I ask him with excitement.

"Yeah. Let's get our coats and go." He tells me. I stand up and slowly walk towards the stairs. Andrew stops me.

"It will be quicker if I run upstairs and grab our coats." He tells me. I nod my head and stand by the stairs. He runs up, grasping the coats and runs down standing next to me. He helps me slide my coat in one arm and drapes it over the other. He then zips my coat up, enclosing my casted arm inside. He places his hand in mine and we walk out to the limo.

The limo drops us off in the front of the entrance of Central Park. Andrew steps out and helps me out. I place my arm in his and we walk down the sidewalk. There are benches and trees everywhere. I exhale as I enjoy the nature walk. We walk for a half hour and I tire quickly, so we sit down at a bench.

"I don't think this was a good idea, your body has been through so much." Andrew says to me worriedly.

"It's fine, Andrew." I tell him. I feel a chill so I place my arm in his, and cuddle close to him for warmth.

"Are you cold?" he asks me. I nod my head. He drapes his arm around me, pulling me close to him. We sit for an hour and then leave.

Andrew helps me up the stairs and to the spare bedroom I was staying in. It was late. I sit on the bed and Andrew sits next to me.

"I'm going to really miss sleeping with you tonight." He says to me.

"Me too, but we don't want to upset your parents." I respond to him. He kisses me on the forehead, and then stands.

"I'll see you in the morning." I nod my head and he leaves, closing my door. I lay on the bed, staring up at the ceiling. I think of Andrew.

I stand up and walk down the hallway towards his room. As I reach his door, it opens and he walks out. He smiles as he sees me standing there.

"I was just coming to you." He says to me with a grin. He moves closer to me, he places his hand on my cheek. I close my eyes, embracing his touch. He places a tender kiss on my lips. I clutch his back, pulling him closer to me. He embraces me tightly and pulls me into his room, closing the door.

As our kisses become more passionate, we tear at each other's clothes until we are standing before each other naked. Andrew scoops me into his arms and gently lies on the bed. He moves atop of me, and places gentle kisses across my face.

"I love you, Jenna." He whispers in my ear.

We make love and lay holding each other. I pull away from Andrew and slide out of the bed, gathering my clothes on the floor. Andrew smiles as he stares at me.

"What are you doing?" he asks me.

"I'm getting dressed and going back to my room. I don't want your parents catching me in your room." I say to him as I slide my panties on.

He jumps out of bed and scoops me into his arms and lies me back on the bed, he lies next to me then slides the covers over us. He wraps his arms around me.

"You are sleeping in my bed tonight, with me." He says cutely.

"Your parents." I tell him.

"Don't worry about them, worry about me. I need to cuddle with you." He says cutely. I cuddle close to him.

I close my eyes and drift off to sleep.

I wake to Andrew placing soft kisses down my neck.

"Good morning." I say to him with a smile.

"It is a very good morning." He responds as he places a quick kiss on my lips.

He stands, extending his hand to me.

"Shower with me." He says softly. I nod taking his hand and we walk to the shower.

Andrew removes my arm splint. He turns on the shower and steps into it, I follow. I place my head under the showerhead, closing my eyes, and letting the water run down my body.

I feel his arms around me. I open my eyes and he places his lips to mine. The fire ignites between us instantly. I want him so bad. I wrap my arms around him, and he pushes me lightly against the tile wall. He lifts me up so I can wrap my legs around him, then he enters inside of me. He carries me, still inside of me over to the bench at the back of the shower sitting down. Slowly he moves me up and down him. I become lost in the ecstasy and throw my head back as I surrender to it. He cups my breasts as his tongue tantalizes my nipples. I build up and I start to move up and down on him faster and faster.

"Oh, Jenna!" he moans. He places his hands on my hips, helping me to move faster.

"Andrew!" I scream. We find our release together. My body goes limp, and he wraps his arms around me, holding me tight to him. He kisses my neck softly.

"I don't know if I can be around you anymore without touching you." Andrew says, breathless. I stare into his eyes.

"I want you to touch me." I respond to him. I slowly move off of him, standing. He stands next to me. My legs shake and Andrew giggles as he notices, standing in front of me.

"I weaken you." he says as he places his hand on my hips, pulling me close. I look up at him as I wrap my arms around his neck.

"You sure do… Now that you made me dirty, I need to shower." I pull away from him and walk over to the running shower head, standing beneath it.

He walks over to me with a washcloth, pouring body wash on it. He washes me from head to toe.

I take the washcloth from him, rinsing it under the shower head. I pour body wash on it and wash him. As I finish washing his leg, I am almost hit in the face by Andrew's very large erection. I stand up, staring at him strangely.

"Seriously does it ever go down?" I ask him shaking my head. He smiles as he pulls me close, rubbing his body against mine.

"It's not me baby… It is you." he responds as he kisses me.

The water was freezing by the time we finally finished showering. Andrew wraps a towel around my head and around my body, and I slide back into bed and under the covers, Andrew follows. He cuddles close to me.

"I'm so cold." he says, shivering as he wraps his cold arms around me.

"It's your fault we took a cold shower." I respond, my lips trembling.

"My fault? It's you and your sexiness."

"Sexiness? That is so generic." I tell him sarcastically.

"What other word would you like me to use, hot? Smoking? Come on Jenna… You know what I mean." he responds as he pulls me closer.

The bedroom door flies open, and William walks into the room. Andrew pulls the blanket up and over me.

"Andrew I went to Jenna's room and she…"—He looks at Andrew and I shocked.

"She's in here." Andrew responds.

"I see that. Well, I uh…" William smiles embarrassed and leaves the room. I face Andrew.

"I just want to die right now." I place a pillow over my face. Andrew removes the pillow from my face.

"It will be fine, don't worry about it." He responds to me. "Come here, I'm still cold." He continues. I cuddle close to him and he smiles.

"There that is better." He says to me. He pulls me closer and I can feel his erection on my leg. I turn to face him.

"Andrew can you not control that thing?" I ask him, giggling.

"I told you it's not me baby, it's you." He responds firmly. He places his lips on mine, kissing me softly.

After we warm up, Andrew walks to his closet and grasps a t-shirt, he walks over to the bed and slides it over my head. I sit on the side of the bed and slide on my panties. I stand up and chuckle as the arms of his t-shirt drapes past my elbows and down past my knees.

"You definitely look better in my shirts than I do." He says to me. I gather my clothes and walk to the bedroom door. I slightly peek out.

"I'm going to make a run for it." I tell him. He laughs loudly and I run out of the room, closing the door.

Andrew dresses and walks down the stairs to the kitchen. His father is sitting at the dining room table reading a newspaper, when

Andrew walks in. He places the newspaper down and looks up at Andrew.

"You and Jenna are awfully cozy." William says to Andrew.

"Yeah." Andrew responds simply. He walks to the coffee pot and pours himself a cup of coffee.

"No matter what Ben does, it still doesn't change the fact that she is married." William continues.

"I am well aware of that, father."

"She is an abused woman, son, with a lot of emotional problems. Are you ready to deal with that?"

"I love her, father." He blurts out. William stares at him distraught.

"No Andrew." William responds in a panic. Wendy walks into the kitchen.

"I love Jenna and she loves me. We are going to be together whether you like or not." Andrew tells him sternly.

"Are you out of your mind? This is not a girl for you." William responds angrily.

Wendy walks up to Andrew, taking his hand in hers.

"Are you sure this is what you want?" Wendy asks him worriedly. He smiles at her.

"I can't breathe if I'm not near her mother. I think about her even when I'm with her. She's amazing and beautiful, inside and out. I need her… I love her." Andrew says to her emotionally. She places her hand on his cheek smiling.

"Then you need to be with her." Wendy tells him. She embraces him tightly.

I interrupt them by walking into the room. A smile instantly encompasses Andrews face.

"Good morning, Jenna." William says to me.

"Good morning." Wendy walks over to me, hugging me.

"Good morning, dear." She says sweetly.

"Good morning." I respond with a smile.

"Are you hungry?" William asks me.

"No." I tell him.

"Yes you are." Andrew says softly. William walks up to me.

"Jenna. I need to ask you what your intentions are when it involves my son." William says to me.

"Jesus father! Nothing like putting her on the spot." Andrew says, embarrassed.

"It's okay Andrew. I don't mind." I say to him with a smile. He mouths the word sorry to me.

"I know that I am married to Ben and this bothers you. When I married Ben, I was young and didn't know really what love was. I thought love was letting him do bad things to me and forgiving him, being told how to dress, how to act, and what to do. But that's not what love is. Love is being there for someone through all the bad times, never giving up on them, and always being there with an open ear, it's enjoying each other. and being happy with what you have together. You ask what my intentions with Andrew are. They are to listen to him, to be with him through the good and through the bad, to love him no matter what comes our way, and to just make him as happy as he makes me. I love your son William, I truly do." Tears fill my eyes, Andrew embraces me tightly.

"I love you, Jenna." He whispers in my ear as he nuzzles his face in my hair.

"I love you too." He drapes his arm around me and turns, facing his father. Tears fall down his father's face.

"Okay then." He says smiling as he sniffles.

Andrew and I eat breakfast then walk to the den. We cuddle close to each other as we watch a movie.

"I really wish we didn't have to leave tomorrow." I tell Andrew.

"I know. Me either." He responds.

It is early afternoon when we arrive back in Michigan. The limo drives down the expressway towards Christie's house. Andrew places his hand in mine.

"Jenna, I want you stay with me at my house." Andrew says out of the blue.

"You mean live together?" I ask him.

"Yes."

"I don't know, don't you think we are moving a little fast?"

"I know it seems like it. But I would feel better if you were with me, with everything going on with Ben."

"What happens if you get sick of me?" I ask him worriedly. He pulls me close to him.

"I could never get sick of you baby, I want to be with you always." He responds, smiling. We pull up in Christie's driveway.

"Okay. But who is going to tell Manny?" I ask him panic stricken.

"I will tell him." Andrew responds to me. We step out of the limo, Andrew places his hand in mine, and we walk into the house.

Andrew takes Manny outside, Christie and I watch as they talk. Manny paces back and forth, throwing his hands up in the air as Andrew stands patiently talking to him. I turn to Christie.

"Do you think Manny is mad?" I ask Christie.

"Not mad, just concerned, Jenna. You are like his daughter; he just doesn't want you to get hurt again." The door wall opens and Manny rushes in walking up to me, Andrew follows.

"What do you want to do, Jenna?" Manny asks me. I stand up and smile at him.

"I love Andrew, Manny. I want to be with him." I tell him. He closes his eyes, exhaling. I look up at Andrew and he smiles.

"I don't know. I am so confused." Manny says as he sits down on the couch. Christie rubs his back.

"Andrew is a good guy Manny, I trust him. I know he will take good care of Jenna." Christie tells him. He turns, smiling at her. He stands up and walks close to me.

"Are you sure this is what you want?" Manny asks me. I nod, smiling.

"Yes." He embraces me tightly.

"Okay. You have my blessing." I kiss him on the cheek.

"Thank you." I take Andrew by the hand and we walk into the bedroom, packing my clothes.

I walk out to the living room and hug Manny tightly.

"I love you Manny."

"I love you too Jenna. If you need me just call." He says tearfully.

"I will." I hug Christie and we leave.

We drive into the driveway of Andrew's house. Andrew grabs two of my suitcases and we walk to the door.

The door opens as we reach it and Eric smiles as he sees me.

"Hi Jenna. What are you doing here?" Eric asks me pleasantly.

"Jenna's going to be staying with us." Andrew tells him. Eric nods and Andrew walks into the house. Matt is lounging on the couch with a girl. He stands up immediately when he sees me. Matisse rushes up to me. I kneel, hugging him.

"I missed you so much, Matisse." I say, hugging him tightly. I stand up.

"What are you doing here Jenna?" Matt asks. happily surprised. Andrew drapes his arm around me.

"She's going to be staying with us." Andrew tells him.

"Like live with us?" Matt asks confused. Andrew places his hand in mine.

"Yes." Andrew responds to him.

Andrew takes my hand and we walk into his room, followed by Matisse. I sit on the bed and Matisse jumps on it.

"Down Matisse." Andrew says sternly. But Matisse doesn't listen. He stretches his body out and whines, laying his head on my lap.

"Leave him alone." I tell Andrew.

"Jenna, he is not supposed to be on the bed."

"He is fine." Andrew shakes his head and walks into the bathroom closing the door.

Eric walks into the bedroom and sits down on the bed next to me.

"So. you and Andrew, huh?" Eric asks me.

"Yeah." I respond smiling.

"Too bad, I was hoping I could take you out." He says flirtatiously.

"You're very sweet, but I am happy with Andrew."

"How does your husband feel about all of this?"

"Who cares what he feels?" Andrew says as he walks into the bedroom. Eric stands up.

"She is his wife, Andrew." Eric says to him worriedly.

"She is my girl now, and that's all that anyone needs to know. I swear, Eric, if you don't stop flirting with my girl, you're going find yourself packing… seriously, cut it out!" Andrew tells him with seriousness.

"Okay, I'm sorry." Eric responds respectfully. He smiles and leaves the room. Andrew sits on the bed and I giggle.

"What is so funny?" he asks me smiling.

"You are so mean to Eric." I tell him.

"It's because he is always flirting with you." he says with frustration.

"I only want you." I say smirking.

He brushes the hair from my forehead. He moves his face closer to mine. Before our lips touch, Matisse jumps in front of us, knocking Andrew backwards. Andrew sits up.

"Matisse cannot be in here." Andrew says sternly.

"Why not?" I ask him sadly. Andrew stands.

"Come Matisse." Andrew says to him. Matisse whines, and moves closer to me. I pet him, smiling.

"Andrew, he is just a baby." I tell him. He shakes his head.

"Matisse now!" he says sternly.

Matisse jumps off the bed and follows Andrew out of the bedroom. I throw my head back on the pillow madly.

Andrew walks into the bedroom and undresses down to his boxers he slides into the bed next to me, cuddling me close. I push him away. He lifts his head.

"You're mad at me because I made the dog leave?" he asks me. I nod my head, pouting. He chuckles. He attempts again to wrap his arms around me and I push him away. He sits up.

"Jenna, stop doing that. I want to hold you." He says with irritation.

"I'm tired, I don't want to be touched." I tell him madly.

He exhales and stands up, sliding his pants on. He leaves the bedroom then comes back a few minutes later with Matisse in tow. I sit up smiling. He slides his pants off and slides into bed. I turn, facing him, smiling. Matisse lies on the floor next to my bed. Andrew wraps his arms around me, and I cuddle close to him.

"Better." He says as he brushes the hair from my face.

"Much." I respond. He places his lips to mine, kissing me. As our kisses become passionate, Andrew slides on top of me. I pull away from him. He looks at me, astounded.

"What's wrong?" he asks me.

"Matisse can see us." I tell him. He shakes his head.

"This is why he should sleep in the utility room." He says with irritation. I shake my head. He stands up and walks to the bathroom.

"Matisse come." He says sternly.

Matisse walks into the bathroom and Andrew closes the door. He runs back to the bed, jumping on me. I laugh at him. He places his lips to mine, kissing me softly.

Andrew falls asleep shortly after we make love. I gently take his arms from around me and walk to the bathroom door, opening it, letting Matisse out. He jumps onto the bed, and I cuddle close to him.

Andrew reaches over to cuddle me and ends up with an armful of fur. He sits up.

"Matisse down!" He says madly. I lift my head turning to him.

"Don't yell at him. It's not his fault. I let him in the bed." I tell Andrew.

"Jenna, I am not sleeping with Matisse every night." Andrew says to me madly.

He stands up, sliding on pajama bottoms and walks to the bathroom. I slide his t-shirt on and walk out to the living room, Matisse follows me. I open the door wall and let him out. I stare out the door wall, watching Matisse. Andrew walks out to the living room.

"Jenna, you can't walk around the house like that, you're practically naked." He says, scolding me. His scolding hurts my feelings. I begin to sob and run to the bedroom, slamming the door. I fall on the bed, crying.

Andrew opens the bedroom door slowly and walks over to the bed sitting down. He picks me up and places me on his lap.

"Hey, don't cry." He says as he wipes the tears from my face.

"I haven't even been here for twenty four hours and all you have done is yelled at me!" I tell him tearfully.

"I'm sorry, baby. I don't mean to yell at you."

"Maybe this was a bad idea, us living together."

"No it wasn't. We just have to get use to each other that is all."

"Okay."

"We have to work together, if this is going to work."

"Okay."

"I don't want Matisse sleeping in our room." He tells me.

"Okay." He looks at me strangely.

"Why are you agreeing with everything I say?"

"I don't want to make you mad." I tell him sadly. He embraces me.

"Jenna, I am not Ben. I am not going to punish you or treat you poorly because you don't agree with me. If we are going to make this work, you have to be honest. I am not perfect, and my opinions are not always correct, okay?"

"Okay." I say with a smile. He hugs me tight.

Living with three men was hard. I was constantly cleaning the house, cooking, and doing laundry. I never returned to work; Andrew felt that it was unsafe for me. I still walked with a slight limp, and had a hard time carrying anything heavy in my right arm from what Ben had done to me, but the doctor told me that in time I would regain full mobility of my arm and leg.

I was finishing dinner when Andrew walks in from work. He walks up behind me, wrapping his arms around me tightly. He lightly rocks me as he holds me close.

"I missed you today." He says to me sweetly. I take the ladle, dip it into the pot, and place it near Andrew's mouth.

"Can you taste this and see if it needs anymore seasoning?" I ask him. He tastes it.

"No. It's really good." He responds to me. I smile and place the ladle down. Eric and Matt walk into the kitchen, they kiss me on the cheek, saying hello.

"You want me to set the table?" Matt asks me.

"Please." I respond to him. He nods and walks to the cupboard.

"I'll grab the salad." Eric says as he opens the fridge.

"Thanks." I tell him. I take Matisse into the utility room and place a plate of beef down and close the door, then walk back to the kitchen.

I had made Beef Stew and a tossed lemon walnut salad. I place the pot on the table, and sit down next to Andrew.

"I hope I find a beautiful girl that can cook and clean like you, Jenna." Matt says sweetly.

"Stop flirting with my girl, Matt." Andrew chimes in madly. I pat his hand.

"Thank you Matt, that is very sweet." I tell him.

After dinner, we all sit in the living room watching movies. Matisse lies next to the couch near me.

Matt invites a girl over, and they cuddle on the couch and then start making out. Andrew stares over at them.

"He should really do that in his bedroom." Andrew says quietly to me.

"Why? They aren't bothering me." I tell Andrew.

"They're bothering me. I don't like that he acts like that in front of you." He says to me.

"What do you mean?" I ask him confused.

"He should have more respect than to be practically doing it with a girl in front of you."

"I don't understand. Is it bothering you, or are you bothered because of me?"

"I'm bothered because of you. I don't want you seeing that."

"Andrew, I am a grown woman. I have done that." He looks at me shocked.

"You have?"

"Yes. I may have only had two men sexually. But I made out with other guys." I tell him. He sits up and looks at me.

"Really?" He says, perturbed. I nod my head and stand up. I walk into the bedroom, and to the bathroom to brush my teeth, Andrew follows me.

"Tell me about these men." He says as he leans against the bathroom door. I finish brushing my teeth and walk into the bedroom, changing into one of Andrew's t-shirts.

"They weren't men, they were boys." I tell him as I slide into bed. He undresses down to his boxers and slides in next to me.

"Ok, well tell me about these boys. How many?" he asks me.

"About six from my freshmen year to my senior year." I tell him.

"Six. What did you do with them?" he asks with interest.

"Mostly just kissing and touching. My senior year, right before I met Ben, there was this one boy. He was so cute and nice. I let him do a little more to me than the others. I really liked him." I explain to him, smiling.

"Exactly what did you let him do?" he asks me. I chuckle.

"What does it matter?" I ask him shaking my head.

"I want to know."

"I let him, you know, put his hands down my pants." I say to Andrew. He moves closer to me, and places his hands in my panties.

"Like this?" he asks as he rubs me softly.

"Mhm." I respond to him. He moves his hand down farther, and places two fingers inside of me.

"Did you let him do this?" he asks me seductively. I shake my head.

"No." I respond, panting as he slowly moves his fingers inside of me. He places his lips to mine and kisses me passionately. He slides his fingers out of me and moves on top of me.

My cell ringing interrupts us. I grasp it and answer it without looking at the number.

"Hello." I answer.

"Hi, darling." Ben says.

"Ben, stop calling me." I tell him, disconcerted. Andrew grabs my cell from me.

"Stop calling her." Andrew says to him madly.

"Well, well. If it isn't the wife stealing attorney." Ben says sarcastically.

"I did not steal her. You lost her because of the way you treated her." Andrew responds instantly.

"You won't win Andrew, I guarantee that. She is mine. Forever… Forever."

"No, she isn't yours anymore. Now stop calling her!" Andrew turns the cell off exhaling. He embraces me tightly. I look at him worriedly.

"It's okay baby."

The morning sun shines brightly through the shutters. I sit up, stretching and yawning as I wake.

Andrew walks around the room, confused. His expression is filled with worry. I stand up and walk up to him.

"What's wrong?" I ask him.

"I have that pain in my stomach again." He says, distraught.

I stroke his face gently.

"You worry too much. Everything will be fine." I tell him. He nods his head. He finishes getting ready for work and we walk out to the living room. He places his hands in mine.

"Jenna please don't answer the door." Andrew says to me worriedly.

"I won't." He embraces me tightly.

"I love you, Jenna."

"I love you too." I respond to him. He releases me and walks to the front door. He looks at Matisse.

"Take care of my girl Matisse." Andrew says to him with a smile. Matisse barks.

I clean the house up and start laundry. I was feeling a little tired so I walk to the bedroom and lie down on the bed. I fall asleep quickly.

"Jenna." I open my sleepy eyes and stare up at Ben. His face wakes me instantly. I sit up, backing up against the headboard, frightened.

"What are you doing here?" I ask him.

"I came to get my wife. It's time to go, darling." He says to me. I shake my head.

"No Ben I'm not your wife anymore, please leave!" I tell him.

"Jenna, let's go." He says to me sternly. I shake my head.

He exhales and places his hand on his belt and unbuckles the gold buckle of the dark brown leather belt, sliding it out. I close my eyes. I hear growling, and open my eyes as Matisse lunges at Ben's hand, the belt falls to the ground, as does Ben. Matisse begins to viciously attack him. I sit, trembling.

Andrew rushes into the bedroom and to me. H embraces me tightly. Detective Mason walks into the room and sees Matisse attacking Ben.

"Can you call your dog off?" He asks us with urgency.

"Matisse." I say tearfully. Matisse releases Ben and jumps onto the bed. I hug him tightly. Andrew pets him.

"Good boy, Matisse." He says to him.

Two police officers pick Ben up from the ground. His face and hands are dripping with blood. Detective Mason walks over to him.

"Let's go, Senator." Detective Mason says to him. They cuff Ben and walk him to the door. He turns and stares at me. Andrew pulls me close to him.

The judge charged Ben with stalking. He also gave Ben 30 days in the county jail for breaking the no contact order.

William was fighting to have the original charges of assault and domestic violence against Ben to be reinvestigated, stating that the prosecutor was a close friend with Ben, and purposely hid crucial evidence. The judge agreed, and a new trial was schedule.

I woke in the morning feeling revitalized. I was finally at peace, knowing that Ben was in jail, and I didn't have to live looking over my shoulder every second of the day.

Andrew woke up late; he rushes out of the bathroom. He runs around the room, looking confused. I watch him and he runs to the closet then to the drawer and back to the closet. He runs back out to the bedroom and notices me smiling. He smiles at me and walks over to the bed. He bends his head and kisses me softly on the lips. As he stands up he gazes at me. I smile with my eyes closed.

"You like that, huh?" He says to me. I nod my head and he bends his head again, kissing me. I wrap my arms around him and pull him on top of me. He lifts his head and smiles at me.

"Do you know how late I am?" he asks me with a raised eyebrow. I nod my head. I place my hand on his head and pull him to me kissing him passionately. He lifts his head. "You are so bad." I pull him close to me again, kissing him.

We make love and shower.

Andrew rushes around the room getting ready, almost in a panic. He stands, fumbling with his tie. I stand up and walk over to him. I take the tie and calmly fix it. He smiles at me.

"Thank you baby."

"You're welcome." He wraps his arms around me, pulling me close, he bends his head kissing me softly. He exhales as he lifts his head.

"Remember, you have a 12:00 appointment with my father today."
"I remember. Manny is going to drive me." I tell him.

"Okay." He kisses me softly on the lips.

"I will see you soon." I nod my head and he leaves.

I had left my car at Christies, and Ben, naturally, re-poed it on me. So I had to find other means to get around. Andrew had offered to purchase me a car, but I felt it was not necessary, being as I didn't have a job.

Manny drives me to the office, dropping me off. I walk up to the information desk. The receptionist smiles at me.

"Can I help you?" she asks me.

"Yes. I am here to see William Carington." I tell her politely.

"I will let Mr. Carington know you are here." She says to me. I nod and walk over to the sitting area, sitting down.

After a few minutes, the receptionist walks over to me.

"Mr. Carington will see you now." The receptionist states. I follow her down the hall. I smile at Andrew as I see him standing in the hall talking to another attorney. He stops us as we pass.

"Where are you going?" he asks me.

"To see your father." I tell him. He turns to the receptionist.

"I'll take her, Jill." He says to her, she nods and leaves. He turns to the attorney.

"I'll catch up with you later." He says to him.

The attorney nods and leaves. Andrew takes my hand and walks me into his office. He closes the door and walks me over to the couch sitting me down, then sits next to me. He drapes his arm around me.

"Why didn't you tell me you were here?" he asks me.

"I was here to see your father. I didn't want to bother you." I tell him.

"You never bother me, baby." He places his lips to mine, kissing me softly.

"You look very professional." He says to me. I was wearing a dark business suit with a white crisp shirt.

"I'm meeting with your father, so I wanted to look professional." I tell him.

Andrew places his hand on my thigh, raising my skirt. He sees the garters and tugs on them.

"Always sexy underneath." He says with a grin. I tap his hand.

"Don't touch." I tell him playfully. He takes his hand and runs it up my thigh again. I tap his hand again.

"No."

"What do you mean no?"

"No. I'm here to see your father. Not to play with you." I tell him sternly. He gently uses his body, pushing me back on the couch.

"You are always available to play with me." He says as he places his lips to mine. He runs his hands up my thigh as he kisses me passionately. His office door opens and he sits up. William walks in smiling.

"Andrew, did you take my 12 o'clock?" William asks jokingly. Andrew stands laughing.

"I had to father. I couldn't resist." Andrew responds jokingly.

"I want her back." His father states with a grin. Andrew laughs. I stand up and Andrew places his hand in mine.

"Are you coming?" I ask him.

"Of course. I want to be involved with anything that concerns you." I nod my head and we walk out of his office to his father's office.

Andrew and I sit on the chairs in front of his father's desk.

"I'm working with the prosecutor. Now we need to let you know, that in order for us to be able to make Ben pay for what he did to you, you are going to have to testify." William says with seriousness.

Andrew stands, shaking his head as he leans over the desk.

"She's not testifying. I don't want her anywhere near him." Andrew sneers.

"Son. There are no witnesses except Jenna. If she doesn't testify, there is a possibility that he will get off."

"Find another way. She's not testifying." Andrew says to him sternly. I place my hand gently on Andrew's arm.

"I can testify." I say to Andrew.

"No Jenna. You've been through enough." Andrew retorts distressed.

"Andrew I don't want him to get away with what he did to me." I tell him desperately. He turns to his father.

"You can find another way." Andrew says to his father.

"Son. There were no witnesses to the attack, the only two people in that room were Jenna and Ben, and he is denying the attack ever happened." He explains passionately.

"You have Eric, Matt, and me. We found her and we can testify to that."

"Son, I have already talked to Eric and Matt, and have their statements. Ben was not there when you found Jenna, and he has an alibi for his whereabouts at the time of the attack."

"All you have to do is have the belt analyzed and match them to the marks on her back. He branded her, find out where he purchased the branding tool that is more than enough proof."

"We need a witness, and unfortunately Jenna is the only witness we have, her testimony will convict him for sure." Andrew paces the room.

"I don't understand why I can't be on this case." Andrew says angrily.

"Son, you know as well as I do, judges despise attorneys who are personally involved with their clients." William says sternly. Andrew exhales nodding his head lightly.

"If her testifying is the only way to put this sadistic bastard away, I guess we will have to do it." William stands.

"I'm going to go down to the prosecutor's office and let them know." He responds to us. He grabs his briefcase and walks out the door.

Andrew and I walk back to his office I sit down on the couch and he sits next to me.

"What do you want to do today?" he asks me. I wrap my arms around his neck, kissing him.

"Oh… I see." He responds with a grin. He pushes me back on the couch and slides atop of me.

The office door opens and Eric walks in. Andrew sits up.

"Do you have a problem with knocking on closed doors?" Andrew asks with frustration.

"Sorry, Kathleen is on line 1, she wants to talk to you." Eric tells Andrew. Andrew nods and stands up walking over to his desk. He picks up the phone.

"Kathleen." He says politely.

Chapter VIII

Andrew chats with Kathleen as I slowly walk gazing around his office, I turn to him and he is watching me with a close eye. I stand in front of the couch and slowly slide my suit jacket off. I slide my shoes off and lie on the couch, stretching my legs out. I tenderly slide my hand up my thigh high exposing my garter, then unclasp it slowly as I stare at Andrew. He smirks as he stares at me. I slide the thigh high off and throw it the ground. I then repeat on the other side.

"I'm sorry Kathleen. I have to call you back." Andrew hangs up the phone and walks over to the couch. He sits down next to me.

"You need me?" he asks me seductively. I nod my head and stand up. I turn so my back is facing him.

Andrew unzips my skirt, sliding it off. Then he stands, sliding off my tank top and smiles when I'm clad only in a corset. I gently push his suit coat off as I kiss him. I unbutton his shirt, sliding it off. He stands quickly and walks to his office door, locking it. He slides out of his pants, only clad in his boxers. He crawls on top of me, kissing me passionately. He stares into my eyes.

"I love you." He murmurs.

We make love and lie on the couch, holding each other.

"I think I want to take you to work with me every day." He says with a smirk. I stand up and slide my tank top on. I pick my skirt up and Andrew grabs me, pulling me back on the couch.

"I'm not done with you yet." I smile at him.

"I can't walk around in your office only wearing a corset and garters." I tell him.

"Yes you can." He says grinning.

"Andrew, you have to work. Now stop, play time is over." He lays me on the couch.

"Stop telling me when play time is over. Play time is over when I am done playing."

"You were spoiled as a child, weren't you?"

"I don't think so."

"Did you have a set play time?"

"No child has a set play time."

"Yes they do. You have to do chores and then homework and then a few hours to play."

"I never did chores, we always had a staff."

"Then that's what's wrong here. You see you have never been taught. There is a time to play, and time to not play. So I will have to be your teacher. Play time is over." I stand up and slide my skirt on. Andrew reaches for me, pulling me back on the couch.

"I was never very good at following the rules, and I definitely don't intend on following them now." He lays me flat and slides on top of me.

"You are definitely going to be put in the corner." I say to him jokingly.

"I will gladly take the punishment for extra play time." He says, smirking. He bends his head, kissing me softly.

I sit with Andrew for an hour longer. Then call Manny to pick me up.

We drive to my house and Manny drops me off.

I begin to do laundry, but Matisse is rambunctious, barking and jumping on me. I decide to take him for a walk to help calm his hyper demeanor.

Matisse and I are strolling down to the park when William calls me. He informs me that Ben and his attorney were there and wanted to meet with him and me.

Apparently, Ben still had some friends left in the court system, as they released him from jail after serving only ten days.

I was desperate to put my past behind, so I agree to meet with them. I take a cab to office. I walk into the office and down the hallway, I run right into Andrew.

"I thought you went home, what are you doing here?" Andrew asks me, confused, but always happy to see me.

"Your father called me in." I tell him.

"Why?"

"Ben and his attorney are here." I say to him.

"Why wouldn't my father tell me that?" Andrew says madly.

"I don't know."

Andrew places his hand in mine and we walk down to William's office. Andrew opens the door. I immediately begin to tremble as I see Ben and his attorney sitting on the chairs in front of William's desk. William stands.

"Father, why didn't you tell me he was here?" Andrew asks William madly. William walks over to him.

"I didn't want to make a scene. I know how much he upsets you." William says to Andrew. Ben stands up, smiling, and walks towards us. Andrew places me protectively behind him.

"Hi darling." Ben says to me as he attempts to tilt his head sideways to see me.

"You stop right there, don't come any closer." Andrew tells him strongly. Ben stops. William stands between Andrew and Ben.

"She is still my wife." Ben says to Andrew.

"No she is not." Andrew tells him.

"We don't have to fight Andrew. We can make this all easy."

"Easy? You think being beaten by you was easy on Jenna?" Andrew asks Ben angrily.

"You have no proof that I did it." Ben responds to him.

Ben's denial infuriates Andrew. He lunges towards Ben and William restrains him.

"Son, this is not the time." William says to Andrew.

"I am taking Jenna out of here." Andrew tells William. He places his hand in mine and walks towards the office door.

"I am prepared to sign the divorce papers." Ben blurts out. Andrew stops and turns facing him.

"In exchange for what?" Andrew asks him. Ben walks closer to us.

"I will plea to non-felonious assault, if you drop the other charges." He says to Andrew.

"You're out of your mind!" Andrew tells him angrily. He turns to walk away.

"You have no proof, you will lose." Ben says to him. Andrew turns to me.

"I need you to stay right here baby, okay." He says to me softly. I nod my head. He releases my hand and walks closer to Ben.

"Do you think for one moment that I am an amateur when it comes to the law? I finished in the top ten of my class and you know why? Because I sleep, eat, and dream the law. I am always one step ahead of you. The scars Jenna bears from your vicious beatings are testimony alone. Where is your belt Ben?" Andrew asks him.

"I am wearing it." Ben responds.

Andrew reaches into the inside of his suit jacket pocket and takes the gold buckle dark brown leather belt out. He throws it at Ben's feet.

"That's your belt. We compared it to pictures of Jenna's marks and it was a perfect match." Andrew tells him.

"That's not my belt."

"Oh yes it is. I have a witness that will testify that it was taken out of your closet and I had it fingerprinted and your fingerprints are all over it."

"So what, that is not enough for a conviction." Ben responds quickly.

"The branding tool is. You are so ignorant; you bought the branding tool with your credit card! We have the credit card receipts to prove it. The fact that you had it specially made with the word MINE on it, the exact words on Jenna's back, is more than enough to prove your guilt!" Andrew explains with a grin.

Ben's face loses all expression. Andrew turns away from him, takes one step, and then turns back around, facing him.

"Oh, and Ben, one more thing; as far as the divorce goes, I am again one step ahead of you. You changed her birth date from May to March, making her only 17 years old at the time you wed. She was underage, and did not have permission from her parents. What you did was fraudulent, which is grounds for an annulment and was final as of 1:00 yesterday. The state will be contacting you about that. I am done talking to you, the next time I want to see you is when they are cuffing you and taking you away." Andrew explains to him. Ben's looks down, distraught. Andrew smiles at him and walks away. He places his hand in mine and we leave the office. We walk into his office, sitting on the couch.

"How did you get his belt?" I ask Andrew, confused.

"Rocco. He felt so guilty about not doing anything when he knew that Ben was beating you. So he came to my office and asked what he could do to help you. I told him I needed the belt. He waited until Ben was asleep and slid into the room, taking the belt from the closet, and then he brought it to me."

"Good ole Rocco." I respond, smiling.

Andrew reaches into his pocket and hands me a picture.

"When I was searching through your school records I found this in an old school yearbook. That's the guy you let put his hands down your pants, isn't it?" Andrew asks me. I chuckle nodding.

"It sure is? How did you know?" I ask him mystified.

"I just knew when I saw his picture."

"Why would you care about him?" I ask as I hand the picture back to him.

"Because I wanted to see my competition, I saw the way your eyes lit up when you talked about him."

"You are so crazy!" I tell him. He wraps his arms around me.

"I am crazy about you." He responds with endearing eyes. He kisses me softly on the lips.

"Why didn't you tell me that I was not married anymore?" I ask him with wonder.

"I wanted to surprise you."

"So I'm single, again."

"No you're not."

"Yes. I am."

"No. You're taken by me." He says, smiling. William walks into the office.

"Why didn't you feel it was necessary to tell me about Ben changing Jenna's birth date? Or that you had Ben's belt?" William asks Andrew.

"Why didn't you tell me Ben was here?" Andrew retorts madly.

"I did not want a scene."

"Do you not know what that man has put Jenna through? How could you put her in the same room as that sadistic bastard?" Andrew asks him angrily.

"I was not thinking." William responds.

"No you weren't." Andrew responds. He stands up and walks over to William.

"Jenna is the woman I love and I will protect her no matter what. I do not want that man near her ever, do you hear me?" Andrew says sternly.

"Yes son. I'm sorry." William says apologetically. Andrew nods and walks back over to the couch sitting down.

"I'm proud of you." William says to him.

"I didn't do it to make you proud. I did it to help Jenna." Andrew responds.

"I know. But I'm still proud of you. You should have seen his attorney's face." William says with a giggle.

"Well, he needs to pay for what he has done to her."

"Yes he does son. And he will." William responds.

I stand up and walk over to William, hugging him.

"Thank you for all your help."

"You are part of our family now; we always take care of our family." Williams says sweetly. "I have an appointment in five minutes. I will see you both later." We both nod and he leaves. I walk back over to the couch and sit down.

"I want to take you somewhere, Jenna." Andrew says to me.

"Okay." I respond. We stand up and he places his hand in mine and we walk out the door.

Andrew drives down the road, past his house, I look at him strangely.

"Where are we going?" I ask him. He smiles but stays silent.

He drives down a dirt road. I can tell it is a trail of some sort, as trees start to close in around us. He stops near a brush. He parks the car and then grabs the blanket from the back. He opens my door and extends his hand to me. I take it and we walk through the brush for fifteen minutes. As it clears I can see a lake below the cliff. I smile at him.

"How did you find this place?" I ask him as I stand, staring out at the breathtaking view. Andrew lays the blanket out and takes my hand. He walks me over to the blanket and sits me down, then drapes his arm around me.

"I know you loved sitting on the cliff looking out at the lake. I wanted to give you place where you could have that, so I found this place for you." He explains to me. I place my hand on his face and tears of joy fill my eyes.

"You did this for me?" I ask him tearfully.

"Yes. I love you, Jenna, and all I want to do is make you happy." He responds to me. I embrace him tightly.

"I love you Andrew, thank you." I respond in a whisper.

We sit silently for an hour, enjoying the serenity of the lake and nature. As night falls, Andrew stands and extends his hand to me. I take it and stand.

"I have one more place to take you." He says to me with a big grin.

"Where are we going?" I ask him with excitement.

"Somewhere special." he responds to me.

He drives into the parking lot of a hotel. He walks over to my door and opens it. He takes my hand helping me out and we walk into the hotel.

Andrew doesn't stop at the desk. He walks down a few doors then takes a key card out of his pocket, sliding in the door. He holds the door open for me and I walk in. I gaze around. The room is filled with candles and rose petals are scattered about the ground. I follow the petals and they lead to a king size bed. Rose petals encompass the whole bed. I stand, staring at it. Andrew takes my hand and walks me to the bed, sitting me down. He walks to the bathroom and opens the door, Matisse runs out.

"Matisse." I say as he jumps onto the bed.

"What is he doing here?" I ask him, smiling.

"I wanted him to be here. I have something I need to ask you." Andrew responds softly.

"Ok. What is it?" I ask inquisitively.

"Jenna, you are my best friend." Andrew says to me.

"You are mine too."

"I love you more than anything." he says nervously.

"I love you too." I respond quickly.

He swallows hard exhaling.

"I need to ask you the most important question I will ever ask anyone." He says trembling. I place my hand on his face gently.

"What is it?" I ask him worriedly.

"I don't like your last name at all." I laugh at his comment.

"Which one, Kramer or Dotson?"

"Neither, I would like to change it, if that's okay?" He says quietly.

He takes my hand and kneels in front of me.

"I promise to always be true to you and put us first. I want to kiss you goodnight, and kiss you good morning for the rest of our lives. I will always listen to you, love you and be there for you. Jenna. I am asking you with all that is my heart to spend forever with me as my wife... Marry me?" Tears fill my eyes instantly, and a smile encompasses my face.

"Oh, Andrew. I don't know what to say."

"Say yes." Andrew responds, smiling.

"Yes... Yes!" I scream. He reaches into his pocket, retrieving an antique silver 4 carat diamond ring. He places the ring on my finger then kisses me.

"I love you." I say to him.

"I love you too." he responds to me. He embraces me, and Matisse jumps on him. As Andrew falls over he pulls me down on the ground. We laugh loudly.

Matisse begins to bark, Andrew tries desperately to calm him down, but the more Andrew attempted to calm him, the more Matisse barked.

A knock at the hotel door brings Andrew to his feet. He stands, talking to a hotel employee, he closes the door when he is finished then walks over to me.

"They're kicking us out. We aren't supposed to have dogs here. I snuck Matisse in." he tells me.

"I don't care, nothing can ruin this night." I kiss him softly. We leave and drive home. I fall asleep on the drive home.

"We're home." He says softly as he strokes my cheek. I stretch and open the car door. We walk into the house and as we turn on the light we are shocked as Matt is on the couch with a girl stark naked having sex. Andrew covers my eyes.

"What the hell are you doing Matt? You have a bedroom!" Andrew says to him angrily.

"Sorry. We didn't make it there." He responds, smiling as he wraps a blanket around him and the girl. Andrew releases his hands from my eyes, shaking his head as we walk to the bedroom. I undress and put one of Andrew's t-shirts on and slide into bed. He is still upset about Matt as he slides into bed next to me.

"I can't believe he was getting it on with that girl right in the open." Andrew says madly. I cuddle close to him.

"Andrew, he's a single young guy, just having fun." I tell him.

"Fun? He has to have some decency." He responds seriously. I chuckle.

"Decency? You think closets, barns, and the conference room at my office is decent?" I ask him. He smirks at me.

"That's different." He responds.

"How so?" I ask him confused.

"Cause we were having an affair. We had to take advantage when we could, where we could."

"I thought it was a one night stand? Not an affair." I say to him jokingly. He pulls me close to him.

"It's more than a one night stand. It's more than an affair." He responds cutely.

"Oh… I see. Everything changes." I tell him smartly. He moves so he's on top of me. "What are you do-"he places his finger on my lips, interrupting me.

"Shh. The only thing I want to do with your lips right now is this." He bends his head and kisses me softly.

William went to court for the stalking charge against Ben, he was found guilty and imprisoned with no bond until the trial.

I wake in the morning, beaming. I stare down at my beautiful engagement ring. Andrew cuddles close to me. He smiles as he sees me staring at my ring.

"You like it?" he asks me.

"I love it, and you." I respond kissing him on the cheek.

"I love you too. I don't want to go to work today." He says as he holds me close.

"Then don't go. Stay home with me." I tell him.

"I wish I could, but I have a very important client I have to meet with today."

"Aww." I respond, pouting. He steps out of bed.

"Shower with me." He says, smiling. We shower and I dress in a pair of sweats and tank top then sit on the bed.

I sit on the bed as Andrew rushes around, getting ready for work.

"Andrew, I want to get a job." I say to him.

"You have a job, you take care of me, Matisse and everyone in this house." He responds as he bends down, picking his shoes up. He sits on the chair and slides his shoes on.

"I'm bored." I say to him.

"Find a hobby."

"Kathleen called me yesterday; she was begging me to come back." I tell him. He shakes his head.

"It's too dangerous, Jenna." He responds worriedly.

"She knows about Ben, she promised she would keep me safe."

"I don't know, Jenna. I get a bad feeling in my stomach about it."

"I want to make my own money."

"You don't need money, I make plenty of it."

"K." I respond pouting. He stands up and walks over to the bed.

"K?" he says to me.

"Are you mad at me?" he asks. I nod my head.

"Yes."

"Why?"

"Because, you are telling me what to do."

"No I'm not. I'm protecting you."

"I'm not a baby." He wraps his arms around me.

"Yes you are. You are my baby." He responds cutely.

"I hate when you do that."

"Do what?"

"Act cute."

"It's not an act." He responds. I push him away.

"You are so conceited."

"No. I'm pretty convinced."

"Whatever." I say, rolling my eyes. He chuckles at my reaction.

"Come on baby, don't be mad." He says, embracing me. I smile at him.

"I can never stay mad at you."

"It's because I'm so cute."

"Whatever… I'm going shopping with Christie today." I say to him.

"Oh, that sounds fun." He responds to me. He kisses me quickly.

"I really have to go. I'll see you tonight after work." He says as he walks to the bedroom door.

"Okay. Bye."

Christie and I shop for hours. I look at the time and it is 6:00. We decide to stop at the pub for a bite to eat, I text Andrew.

"Christie and I are going to the pub for dinner." I text him.

"Ok baby, have fun. I will see you when you get home."

"Okay. Love you."

"Love you too."

We eat and then order a few cocktails. Christie and I are having such a great time I don't even realize how late it is. I become inebriated and we walk to the dance floor and start dancing. A couple of men walk over to us on the dance floor, and start dancing with us.

"Jenna." I turn and Andrew is standing in front of the dance floor.

"Hi." I say as I walk up to him.

"Do you know what time it is?" he asks me.

"No." I respond to him. He stares at Christie and notices that we are both intoxicated. He walks out to the dance floor, and gently takes Christie by the hand.

"Come on, Christie, I will drive you home." Andrew says to her.

"Okay." She responds happily. We walk out to the car. Andrew drives to Christies and walks her up to the house. Manny opens the door.

"She was too drunk to drive her car; it's still at the Pub." Andrew tells Manny.

"Thanks a lot Andrew." Manny says to him with a smile.

"No problem." Andrew responds. Manny walks Christie into the house. Andrew walks back to the car. I pass out as we drive home. Andrew carries me into the house and lies me on the bed.

I wake in the morning to my stomach twirling. I jump out of bed and rush to the bathroom, vomiting. Andrew holds my hair and rubs my back.

After I finish vomiting, I lie on the cool bathroom floor. Andrew scoops me up in his arm and carries me back to bed.

I sleep for a few more hours.

My eyes wake and I sit up slowly, attempting not to erupt my impending hangover. Andrew is sitting on the chair at the end of the bed, tapping his foot.

"What?" I ask him as he glares at me. He throws a crumpled piece of paper on the bed. I reach for it and read it. The name Christopher is written on it with a phone number. I throw it down.

"I don't know where that came from." I say to him. I lie back on the pillow.

"I'll tell you where it came from. When I undressed you, because you were too drunk to undress yourself, it fell out of your bra." He says to me madly.

"I really don't know where it came from." I say to him.

"Where's your ring, Jenna?" he asks me. I look at my hand and my engagement ring is missing. I sit up.

"I don't know." I say to him worriedly. He holds the ring up as he walks to the bed, sitting down.

"This was in your purse. Why would you take your ring off?" Andrew asks me.

"I don't know. I don't know, Andrew. I'm telling the truth." I say to him, confused.

"Do you want to be with me, Jenna?" Andrew asks me hurtfully.

"Of course I do." I respond to him.

"Then why did you take your engagement ring off, and why do you have another man's number…in your bra?" he asks me.

"I don't know. I really don't." I say to him. He exhales. I wrap my arms around his neck and lie down, pulling him on top of me.

"I love you, Andrew. I would never be untrue to you." I say to him with a smile.

"I love you too, Jenna. I just always want you to be honest with me. I don't like feeling like I'm being lied to."

"I am not lying to you." I respond. He nods and kisses me on the lips. I smile keeping my eyes close.

"You like that, huh?" He says with a chuckle. I nod my head. He bends his head, kissing me again. I pull him close to me, and our kisses become passionate. The bedroom door opening interrupts us. Andrew sits up instantly and I sit next to him.

"Sorry, I didn't mean to interrupt. But we have to go; we have to meet that client in fifteen minutes." Eric says to Andrew. Andrew nods and Eric leaves.

Andrew places his hand in mine and slides my engagement ring back on my finger.

"Do not take this off." He says to me sternly. I nod, smiling. He kisses me quickly.

"I'll see you tonight."

"Ok." He stands up and leaves.

I shower then walk around the house, straightening up. I gather the laundry from all the bedrooms then walk to the laundry room and separate it. Matisse barks at the door wall, so I walk over, letting him out. I then walk back to the laundry room and place a load in. As I start the washer Christie calls me.

"Hello." Christie says to me.

"Jenna, remember those two guys we met last night, well the guy I was talking to Charlie, he called me and they want to meet us again." Christie says with excitement.

"Christie I don't remember anything last night. Andrew found a number in my bra and my engagement ring was in my purse." I respond to her.

"I put the number in your bra and I took your engagement ring off."

"Why would you do that? Do you know how pissed off Andrew was?"

"I was having a lot of fun with that guy, Jenna. And I knew if his friend thought you were engaged he wouldn't talk to you. He handed you his number and you left it on the table. He saw it on the table and looked sad, so when he turned I grabbed it and slid it in your shirt. It must have slid into your bra by accident."

"You are married to Manny." I tell her sadly.

"All Manny does is play hockey and work. He's dull. I want to have fun."

"Come on Christie, I love Manny."

"Come with me tonight and meet those guys."

"I'm engaged."

"You don't have to do anything with him. Just talk to him so I can see his friend."

"I don't know Christie, Andrew isn't too happy with me right now."

"Please." I sit silently contemplating what to do.

"Okay, but you can't tell Andrew we are meeting them."

"Okay. I won't I promise. I'll pick you up at 8."

"Okay."

I sit, pondering with my thoughts. I knew that Andrew would not be too happy about me going out again. I decide to test the waters and text him.

"Andrew, my sister wants me to go out with her tonight."

"Again?"

"Yes. Just to the Pub."

"You are a grown up. I can't tell you what to do, but I will tell you this, I am not feeling too comfortable with it."

"We're just hanging out. I promise I won't be too late."

"I guess."

"Thank you." I place my cell in my purse.

Andrew sits on the couch as I finish getting ready. I walk out to the living room and sit down next to him.

"You look very pretty." He says with a big smile.

"Thank you." I respond. I kiss him softly. He wraps his arms around me.

"Why don't you stay home with me?" He says as he nuzzles his face in my hair.

The doorbell rings and Matt answers. Christie walks in. I look at her, shocked. She is wearing a half-top with a skirt so short you can practically see her panties. I turn to Andrew, and he looks at me, surprised.

"Are you hiding something from me?" Andrew asks me suspiciously.

"No." I respond, smiling. I kiss him.

"I won't be late." I tell him.

"Have fun." I walk over to Christie and we leave.

Charlie and Christopher are waiting for us at a table when we walk in. I sit and talk to Christopher. Charlie and Christie take off after an hour; I become worried.

"Where are they?" I ask Christopher.

"Don't worry about them. They are just having fun." Christopher responds. He notices my engagement ring.

"Are you engaged?" he asks me. I nod my head. He stands up.

"He tricked me again." Christopher says as he walks away.

I sit at the table alone, and after two hours I become worried. I call Andrew and he drives up to the Pub. I wait outside for him. He walks up to me.

"What is going on?" he asks me.

"Christie took off with a guy." I tell him.

"What do you mean?" he asks me. I exhale. "Jenna, tell me what's going on.

I tell Andrew everything. About Christie and Charlie, and how she was the one that took my engagement ring off and placed the number in my bra. I also tell him about how Christie wanted me to come to hang out with Charlie's friend Christopher, so she could hang out with Charlie.

"So you came with her, knowing you were going to hang out with this guys friend?" he asks me madly. I nod. He shakes his head.

"How could you do that?"

"I'm sorry." Christie walks up hand in hand with Charlie she sees Andrew and pulls away from him.

"What are you doing Christie?" Andrew asks her madly.

"Andrew, stay out of it." Christie tells him.

"I am not. Manny is my friend, how could you do this to him?" Andrew asks her.

"I'll talk to you later, Charlie." Christie says to him, Charlie walks away.

"Look Andrew, you are not exactly a saint. I clearly remember you sleeping around with my sister when she was very married to Ben." She continues.

"You know damn well that was a totally different situation." Andrew says defensively.

"I'm going home. I have to work in the morning. I will call you later, Jenna." Christie says to me and walks away.

Andrew and I drive home. He stares at the road avoiding eye contact with me. I place my hand on his, rubbing it gently.

"Are you mad at me?" I ask him.

"Yes."

"I'm sorry."

"I don't think you really understand what you are doing. I know you were helping your sister out, but what if this guy would have found out that you were leading him on, men don't like to be lead on, Jenna. You could have put yourself in a very bad situation." He preaches.

"I told him I was engaged, Andrew." My words don't comfort him; they just make him more angry. He exhales

"Let's just drop it."

"Okay."

We drive into the driveway then walk into the house. I ready myself for bed. I walk into the bedroom and Andrew is already in bed. I slide in next to him and he rolls over, away from me. I exhale and curl to my pillow.

Andrew is gone when I wake in the morning. He was still very upset with me. I do my daily duties and then start dinner. My phone buzzes and I stare down at it.

"I have to work late tonight. I don't know what time I will be home." Andrew texts.

"Ok. I love you." I text back. He doesn't reply and I place my cell on the counter.

I lie on the bed and wait for Andrew. I look at the time it is already 1:00 am. I curl to my pillow and fall asleep.

I wake in the morning and turn to my side and Andrew is not there. The blanket is still made on his side, indicating he had not been home all night. I walk out in the living room, hoping he had fallen asleep on the couch, but he is nowhere in the house.

All day the anger builds inside of me, as Andrew does not contact me. When 6:00 comes and goes I am so infuriated I am ready to explode. I grasp my cell and call him; his phone goes straight to voicemail. It was happening again, just like with Ben.

Christie calls me at 8:00.

"Can you get out?" she asks me.

"Yes."

"Do you want me to pick you up?"

"No I will meet you there." I tell her.

I hurry up and get ready and call a cab.

As soon as I get to the pub, I begin to drink and drink, until I can't drink anymore. Christopher asks me to dance and I accept. I stumble out to the dance floor and he wraps his arms around me. We are dancing when I feel my body leave the ground. I turn and Andrew is holding me close to him.

"What are you doing?" he asks me angrily. Christopher walks up to us.

"Let her go." Christopher says to him.

"Christopher?" Andrew asks him.

"Yes." Christopher responds.

"I am her fiancée, I suggest you beat it." Andrew tells him angrily. Christopher throws his hands up in the air and walks away. I pull away from Andrew.

"Let me go." I say to him angrily. I stumble back onto the dance floor. Andrew scoops me up into his arms.

"It's time to go home." He says to me. I start hitting him as he carries me out of the Pub.

"Put me down!" I scream madly at him. Manny is sitting in the car in front of the Pub, Christie is in the passenger side and they are arguing. Andrew places me in the back seat of his car and closes the door. I grasp the handle, attempting to escape. He grabs my hands and I start hitting him.

"Let me out!" I yell.

"No." he responds to me. He embraces me.

"Let me go."

"No." He responds madly.

Chapter IX

Manny drives us to the house. Andrew slides out, and then reaches in for me. I back away to the door, avoiding his reach. He climbs in and gently wraps his arms around me, pulling me to the door. I hit him as he takes my hand in his and pulls me out of the car.

"I'm not going with you!" I yell madly as I pull away from him.

"Jenna please, you have been drinking, and you don't know what you're saying." Andrew responds.

"I am not going with you!" I repeat. His patience has reached its limits.

"Oh yes you are!" He responds with irritation

"If she doesn't want to go with you, she doesn't have to!" Christie screams with infuriation out the window.

"Stay out of it, Christie, we have our own problems!" Manny tells her sternly.

Andrew scoops me into his arms and carries me into the house. He stands me up, releasing me as he closes the front door. I run to the bedroom and slam the door, locking it. Andrew pounds on the door.

"Open the door, Jenna!" He yells with frustration.

"No. Go away and leave me alone!" I yell back. He kicks the door a few times then it flies open. I jump on the bed and he walks up to me. He stares at me angrily.

"What are you going to do hit me? Beat me like Ben did?" I ask him, sneering. He sits next to me. I hit him and he lies on top of me, restraining my body with his.

"Settle down!" He says to me.

"Get off of me!" I respond to him.

"No." he says sternly.

"So are you going to force yourself on me?" I ask him.

"I would never do that." He responds distraught.

"Get off of me." I start to sob.

"No." he says softly. I start to sob harder, and he strokes my head gently.

"Please don't cry." He says to me emotionally.

"You are just like Ben! Why don't you just get it over with and hit me, it would hurt less?" I respond tearfully.

"I am not Ben." He responds, disconcerted.

"You left me alone all night and all day, you didn't call, who is she?" I ask him, sobbing.

"Jenna, there is no one else, only you."

"You're lying… you're lying!" I respond, still sobbing. He embraces me.

"No baby, I'm not lying. I wasn't with a girl, I was with Manny. He is going through a hard time with Christie. I lost track of time. I fell asleep at his house. And was there all day, I didn't have my charger and my phone went dead."

"Why didn't you use his phone?" I ask him, sniffling.

"He doesn't have one anymore. When Christie came home the other night, she made him so mad he threw it into the wall." I still didn't believe him. I pull away from him, curling to the pillow.

"Please just leave me alone." I tell him, still sobbing.

"Never. I will never leave you alone." He responds softly. He embraces me tightly. "I love you baby, only you. I would never be untrue to you." He continues. I turn to face him and look into his eyes, and can tell he's being truthful.

"Oh Andrew, I'm sorry I'm such a mess." I say, sobbing.

"You are not a mess. You have had a lot of bad stuff happen to you, it's not your fault." He brushes the hair from my face, kissing me softly. I close my eyes and embrace him tightly.

"Don't ever leave me. Please don't ever leave me."

"I will never leave you, I promise."

"I'm sorry I hit you."

"It's okay, I understand, you were very upset." We lay down on the bed.

"When I saw you with that guy dancing, I almost lost it. Jenna, it's not okay for you to dance with other men. How would you feel if you walked in somewhere and I was dancing with other women?"

"I wouldn't like it."

"So, no more dancing with strange men, okay?" He says, wanting a reply.

"Okay."

"I love you."

"I love you too." He cuddles close to me and we fall asleep quickly.

Andrew's firm had a big benefit that we had to attend. I finish dressing, wearing a long black sequenced evening gown with a slit up the side. I walk out to the living room where Andrew is waiting for me. He smiles as I walk up to him.

"You look beautiful." He says kissing me on the cheek. He was dressed in a black tuxedo with a matching bow tie.

"You don't look so bad yourself." I tell him as I straighten his tie. I kiss him softly on the lips.

"Maybe we should stay home." He says as he kisses my neck softly.

"We have to go." I tell him. He nods his head and we leave.

The limos lined up in the front of the benefit. Andrew steps out of the limo, extending his hand to mine. I take it and we walk into the benefit. Kelly walks up to us immediately, she hugs Andrew tightly, taking him by surprise.

"Hi Kelly." Andrew says as he pulls away from her. She smiles at me.

"Hi Mrs. Kramer." Kelly says to me pleasantly.

"Hi." I respond to her. Andrew places his hand in mine, which surprises Kelly.

"Wait, you two?" She questions. Andrew nods as he drapes his arm around me proudly.

"Yes. We are engaged." He tells her happily. She shakes her head.

"Well. Congratulations!" She says with a smile.

"Thank you." Andrew responds. We walk into the benefit and Andrew is immediately whisked away by his father to meet important clients. I walk to the bar, sit down, and order a Margarita. I sit, waiting for Andrew, and don't realize until I stand to walk to the bathroom that I had drank a little too much. I stumble, holding on to the walls as I make my way to the bathroom. I walk down the hall and turn the corner and see Andrew and Kelly talking quietly in the corner. I stand, staring at them. Andrew is laughing and enjoying himself; the calmest I had ever seen him. I quietly turn and walk away.

The hurt fills me as the realization of all the drama in my life had been the only foundation that Andrew and I's relationship had been built on. In my inebriated state, I stumble and almost fall when a man catches me.

"Whoa you have to watch yourself." He says sweetly. He stands me upright.

"Excuse me. I'm so sorry." I say to him, apologetic.

"It's fine. I'm Doug." He says, extending his hand out to me.

"I'm Jenna." I tell him, shaking his hand

"Would you like to dance Jenna?" Doug asks me. I think for a moment, and flashes of Andrew and Kelly run through my mind. I face Doug, smiling.

"Yes." He takes my hand and we walk out to the dance floor. We sway to the music and make small talk. I stare out at the people and my eyes stop as I see Andrew. He glares at me madly. I turn my head and begin talking to Doug.

"So Doug, are you an attorney?" I ask him.

"Yes. I am with the Downing firm." He answers.

Doug's hand slides down my back and he places it gently on my behind. I know I should have stopped him, but my mind is running slow in my inebriated state. Before I could say anything Andrew is next to us. He taps Doug on the shoulder. Doug turns to him.

"Do you want to take your hands off of my fiancée?" Andrew asks him angrily. Doug removes his hands from me.

"I'm sorry Andrew. I didn't know she was your fiancée." Doug says instantly. Andrew walks up to me, taking my hand in his.

"It's okay Doug." He responds. He pulls me off the dance floor. I stop, yanking my hand from him.

"Don't touch me!" I tell him. He shakes his head and wraps his arms around me.

"I thought we just had this conversation about you dancing with other men." He tells me madly. I pull away from him and walk towards the door. He walks behind me and reaches, grabbing my hand, pulling me to him.

"What's wrong with you?" Andrew asks me. I push him away and turn, walking away again. He rushes up to me and grabs my hand again.

"Let me go!" I say madly, pulling my hand from his.

"What is your problem Jenna?" Andrew asks me confused.

"Why don't you go harass Kelly? It seems you two were having a great time, in the corner." I tell him. He wraps his arms around me.

"You're jealous. I assure you I don't want Kelly. I only want you." I push him off of me.

"You could have fooled me." I run out of the benefit and through the front door. Andrew chases after me. He wraps his arms around me tightly. I attempt to pull away from him but he just tightens his hold on me.

"Please Andrew let me go!" I say to him tearfully.

"No Jenna. I'm never letting you go." He responds to me. He waves his hand in the air and a limo pulls up. He walks me to the limo and gently places me inside. I slide across it, grasping the opposite door wanting to escape. Andrew grabs me and pulls me close to him. I start to hit him.

"Don't touch me!" I scream He grabs my hands. "Let me go!" I scream.

"Then stop hitting me." He responds madly. I calm down and sit back on the seat and stare out the window. Andrew releases my hands.

The house is dark as we walk in. I turn on the light and walk silently to the living room. I sit down on the couch and stare out the window. Andrew sits down across from me.

"Talk to me, Jenna." He says softly. I shake my head.

"I have nothing to say." I tell him. He stands up and sits down next to me. He turns me to face him.

"Kelly is a friend, Jenna that's all." He says to me. Tears start to fall down my face as I look at him.

"You don't get it. You don't understand at all." I tell him tearfully. He wipes my tears and brushes the hair back from my face.

"Make me understand. Please talk to me." He pleads.

"When I saw you two together you looked so happy, so calm. Our relationship has been built around you taking care of me, protecting me from Ben. You deserve to have a normal life, not having to deal with all the drama in my life." I explain to him tearfully.

"So you think I would be happier with Kelly?"

"Yes." He shakes his head.

"No Jenna. I don't think you understand. Until I met you I didn't know what it was like to need someone as much as I need you. I didn't know what it was like to care and love someone as deeply as I love you. I know it has been rough and our relationship isn't as normal as it should be. But I would deal with a hundred Ben's and everything that comes along, if I knew it would lead me to you. Because you are the one for me, you will always be the one for me." He explains with endearing eyes. I lunge at him, embracing him tightly.

"I love you so much Andrew." He embraces me back.

"Oh baby, I love you." He bends his head kissing me softly.

He scoops me into his arms, his lips never leaving mine, and carries me to the bedroom. He stands me in front of the bed. He smiles as he stares at me. He unzips my dress and gently pushes it off my shoulders, letting it fall to the ground. I stand, clad only in my corset and panties. I unbutton his shirt and push it off of his shoulders, letting it fall to the ground. I kneel and slide his pants down, removing his boxers. I smile as I look up at him and wrap my hand around him and take him in my mouth. He closes his eyes and moans as I slowly slide my mouth across him. Before I am finished, he lifts me gently.

"I want to make love to you." He says to me. He takes my hand and walks me to the bed. I slide onto it. He crawls between my legs, placing my hands in his he pulls me up, unclasping my corset. Then he lies me down and moves to my panties, sliding them slowly off. He kisses my calves and moves slowly up to my thigh. I am building up as he lightly kisses my stomach. Then he moves to my breasts, tantalizing my nipples with his tongue.

"Oh!" I moan loudly. He kisses my neck and then places his lips to mine softly. He enters me and moves slowly. My hips move in sync with his. He begins to pick up the pace and I wrap my legs in his.

"Oh Oh Andrew!" I scream and he comes undone.

"Jenna…. Jenna!" he screams as he moves faster inside of me. I find my release instantly. Andrew places tender kisses across my face as he wraps his arms around me. I fall asleep in the comfort of his arms.

It took a lot of pleading and convincing, but I was able to finally talk Andrew into allowing me to go back to work for Kathleen. I rushed around the bedroom, getting ready for work. Andrew walks out of the bathroom, smiling. I walk up to him, embracing him tightly.

"I am so excited!" I say to him.

"I want you to be careful." He responds to me. He walks over to his nightstand and retrieves a gun. He hands it to me.

"Put this in your purse, just in case." He says to me. I nod my head and place the gun in a secret pocket in my purse.

"I don't understand why you are so worried about it, you are working there today, right?" I ask him.

"Yes but I still can't help but worry. I told you I get this pain in my stomach when I feel like something is wrong, and I have it right now."

"You worry too much." I respond to him. He wraps his arms around my waist, pulling me close to him.

"Don't you think I have reason to worry?"

"I suppose."

"Until Ben Kramer is locked up, I will worry." He kisses me quickly. "We have to get going." He tells me. I nod my head and we leave.

Andrew and I drive to the office. As we walk inside, we separate, he walks into the conference room and I walk upstairs to my desk. Stacks of papers encompass my desk, and I could tell, since I had been gone no one was keeping up with my work. I turn on my computer, and, one by one, I go through the stacks of papers.

I worked diligently, attempting to catch up. Andrew walks into my office. He sits on the desk. I look up from my computer, smiling at him. He rubs my back gently.

"How are you doing?" he asks me.

"Busy." I answer. He smiles and bends kissing me. I close my eyes, smiling. He lifts his head and smiles.

"You like that, huh?" he asks me. I nod, still smiling. He bends his head, kissing me again. I wrap my arms around him, wanting more. He pulls me out of my chair, leaning me against the office door. Our kisses become passionate quickly. He pulls my skirt up rubs my butt softly.

"I want you so bad." He says, panting in my ear. I place my lips to his, and then blindly lock the door. I pull myself up on him, wrapping my legs around him. He carries me to an open area, and lies on the ground with my legs still wrapped around him. A knock at the door interrupts us. We pull away from each other, standing quickly. I pull my skirt down and rush over to my desk, sitting. Andrew smiles at me, then walks to the door, unlocking it. It's Eric.

"Hey. We have some problems. The reports aren't matching up." Eric tells him.

"I'll be right down." Andrew says to him. Eric nods and leaves. Andrew walks up to me, smiling. I look up at him.

"Can I take a rain check?" he asks me with a half-lipped smile. I nod my head. He kisses me quickly and leaves.

I probably would have worked into the next day if Andrew wouldn't have walked upstairs to fetch me.

"Come on baby, it's late." He says to me. I shut down my computer and we leave. As soon as we get home I start dinner. Eric and Matt walk in the house immediately after us. Eric walks into the kitchen and kisses me on the cheek.

"Do you need any help, Jenna?" Eric asks me.

"No I got it, thanks for asking." I respond. He nods his head and leaves. I call everyone to the dining room as I place dinner on the table. I am surprised to see an extra face at the table. I smile at her.

"Hi." I say pleasantly. She is cute with short reddish hair and big turquoise eyes. It's obvious she is wearing colored contacts.

"Hi." She responds happily

"This is Marnie." Matt says proudly.

"Hi Marnie." I respond. Andrew walks to the table and notices Marnie.

"Hi." He says to her.

"Hi." She responds.

"This is Marnie." Matt tells Andrew. Andrew sits down and I sit next to him. Andrew nods.

"I'm starving." Andrew says aloud. He grabs the salad and puts some in his bowl and some in mine. I grab the platter of Chicken breasts, and place one on his plate and one on mine.

"Thank you." Andrew says, smiling. I smile back. I turn and face Marnie.

"So Marnie what do you do?" I ask her.

"I work for Senator Kramer." She says nonchalantly. My heart begins to beat fast. Andrew rubs my back gently.

"It's okay, Jenna. A lot of people work at his office." Andrew responds.

"I'm sorry Jenna, I didn't know." Matt chimes in.

"It's okay." I respond quickly.

"What's wrong?" Marnie asks Matt confused.

"Jenna was married to him." Matt tells her.

"You are the Mrs. Kramer he boasts about all the time." Marnie says to us. I nod and look down at my chicken breast, cutting it up into little pieces.

"What does he say?" Andrew asks with interest.

"That some attorney brainwashed his wife and stole her from him, and that he's going to get her back someday." Marnie explains.

"If anyone brainwashed anyone, it was him brainwashing Jenna!" Andrew blurts out angrily to Marnie. I place my hand on his and rub it gently.

"It's not her fault." I tell him.

"You're right. I apologize, Marnie." Andrew says softly.

"I understand. So, you must be the attorney?" She says with a smile.

"Yes. I am." He responds, smiling back.

"And he's not brainwashing me either. I am here because I want to be." I say to her. Andrew smiles at my comment.

After dinner, we all sit around and watch a movie. Marnie invites a friend of hers over and Eric snuggles close to her on the couch. Matt is different with Marnie, he holds her hand but makes no attempt to maul her like he had a habit of doing with the other girls.

"I think he really likes this girl." I whisper to Andrew.

"Why do you think that?" Andrew asks me.

"Because, he's not all over her." I respond, laughing. Andrew gazes over at Matt.

"I think you might be right. Thank god, I can't take anymore naked women on my couches." He responds jokingly.

"You don't like naked women on your couches?" I ask him with a raised eyebrow.

"Only you, baby." He responds with a smirk.

We finish watching the movie, and excuse ourselves to bed. The day was exhausting for me, so I fall asleep immediately.

I wake in the middle of the night to the pounding of the front door. I naturally sit up and Andrew sits up next to me.

"Stay here. I'll go see who it is." Andrew says. He slides out of bed and slides on a pair of flannel pajama bottoms and leaves the room. He walks back in a few minutes later.

"It's Christie." He says to me. I stand up and throw on a pair of sweats and walk out to the living room, Andrew follows. Christie is sitting on the couch, sobbing. I sit down next to her, and embrace her tightly.

"I messed up so bad, Jenna." She says to me. Andrew sits on the couch across from us.

"What happened?" I ask her with concern.

"I met Charlie tonight, and Manny followed me. They ended up in a huge fight and Manny beat him up." I tell her.

"I'm sorry Christie." I hug her tightly.

"A knock at the door brings Andrew to his feet; he walks over to it, answering it.

"Where is she?" Manny asks Andrew as he walks into the house. Andrew points to the living room and Manny walks over to us.

"I'm not talking to you, Manny." Christie says to him instantly.

"Christie, what did you expect me to do? You are my wife running around with some guy!" Manny tells her.

"You didn't have to hurt him. He didn't do anything wrong." Christie says to him angrily. She stands up

"Are you fucking kidding me? He's running around with my wife! I already warned him once!" Manny responds, screaming. Andrew walks over to him.

"Calm down, Manny." Andrew pats him on the shoulder attempting to calm Manny.

"You don't understand, Andrew. I love her more than anything and I don't understand what she needs from this guy." Manny says, upset.

"He pays attention to me. You work, play hockey, and don't give me any of your time." Christie tells Manny.

"Is that what it is?" Manny asks Christie. She nods her head and he walks closer to her. He places his hands on her arms.

"Why didn't you tell me?" Manny asks her.

"I didn't want to be that wife that nagged for her husband's time. I just wanted you to want to spend time with me." She explains to him. He embraces her tightly.

"Christie you are my life. If you were unhappy you should have told me. Hockey is not as important to me as you are." He responds to her.

"Really?"

"Yes. I love you."

"Oh Manny, I love you too." She embraces him tightly. I stand up and walk over to Andrew, he drapes his arm around me.

"Let's go home and talk about it, okay?" Manny says to her.

"Okay." They walk towards the front door.

"Thanks for everything." Christie says to us. We both nod and they leave.

Andrew and I walk to the bedroom and slide into bed. He wraps his arms around me, cuddling me close, and we drift back off to sleep.

I rush around the room getting ready for work. It was one of those days where no matter how hard I attempted to ready myself; I just couldn't complete the task. Andrew walks over to me as I am sliding my thigh highs up.

"Let me help you with that." He says, smirking. He kneels in front of me and attaches my thigh highs to my garters. He runs his hand up my thigh softly.

"Andrew, I don't have time to play today." I say to him.

"You always have time to play with me." He responds as he runs both of his hands up my thighs.

"I really don't." I tell him sternly. I stand up and walk into the bathroom, he follows me. I stand in front of the mirror, applying my makeup. He walks behind me, wrapping his arms around me.

"Andrew I really can't we are going to be late." I tell him. He scoops me into his arms and carries me to the bedroom, laying me on the bed. He smiles as he crawls on top of me.

"Isn't a few minutes of being late worth the grin I will have on my face all day?" he asks me. I laugh at his comment. He places his lips to mine.

I rush into the bathroom after we make love. Applying my makeup quickly and fixing my hair.

Andrew parks in the office parking lot, and I run up to the door. I walk in and am met immediately by Kathleen. She gazes at her watch.

"You are late." She says to me.

"Sorry." I respond to her. She nods her head and walks away. Andrew walks into the office.

"See, no big deal." He says to me with a grin. I playfully hit him and make my way up to my office.

We finish our day and travel home.

After dinner, I walk to the bedroom and Matisse follows me. Andrew works in the den, finishing paperwork he was behind on. He walks in the bedroom and stops by the door, smiling as he sees me and Matisse asleep on the bed. He walks over to the bed and Matisse sits up, growling at him. As Andrew walks closer he starts barking. It wakes me; I sit up and rub his side gently.

"It's okay Matisse, it's Andrew." I say to him sleepily. Andrew walks closer and Matisse growls.

"Jenna, I think you are going to have to put him in the utility room. He's not going to let me near him." Andrew explains. I nod my head and step out of the bed, walking towards the utility room, Matisse follows me. I place him in the utility room. I kiss him and hug him tightly then close the door. I walk back to the bedroom and slide into the bed. Andrew slides in beside me, cuddling me close.

Matisse whined all night for me. I finally caved in and walked to the utility room.

Andrew moves to cuddle me and I am not there. He sits up and looks around the room. He walks into the bathroom and sees I'm not there. He walks through the living room and to the utility room, opening the door. He stands by the door smiling as he sees me cuddled up to Matisse. He quietly walks in the room. Matisse lifts his head and Andrew scoops me into his arms, carrying me back to the bedroom. I wake as he lays me on the bed. Matisse jumps up on the bed. I look at Andrew.

"I would rather have you in the bed with him, then not have you in bed with me at all. But you're sleeping in the middle; I am not cuddling a dog." He says to me. I smile and I jump in between Matisse and Andrew. Andrew wraps his arms around me and we drift off to sleep.

After I shower I walk over to the bed and Matisse is lying down. I sit next to him and he looks at me sadly. I pet his head and he whines.

"I think he's depressed." I tell Andrew. He sits on the chair sliding his shoes on.

"Why would he be depressed? He gets more of your attention than I do." Andrew says madly. I walk up to him.

"What's wrong?" I ask him.

"You give all your attention to him." He stands up and walks to the bathroom.

"Andrew you're not jealous of Matisse, are you?"

"Yes. I am." I wrap my arms around his neck.

"He just needs me right now; he's going through some kind of doggie depression." I tell him.

"Jenna, I need more of your attention, that's all I'm saying."

"Okay." I smile kissing him quickly.

I call Kathleen as Andrew is getting ready. I didn't feel comfortable leaving Matisse alone with his depression. Andrew and I drive to work and Matisse sits in the middle. I could see it was aggravating Andrew.

"Are we now a threesome?" he asks me with irritation.

"It's just for now until he gets through his depression." I tell him. He exhales with frustration.

We walk into the office and Kathleen rushes up to us right away.

"When you said you were bringing your dog to work I expected a Pomeranian or a shiatsu not a baby bear!" she says, astounded.

"He's really friendly. I promise he will stay in my office the whole time." I tell her. She nods hesitantly and walks away. Evan walks up and Matisse lets out a large bark and then pounces on Evan.

"Off, Matisse!" I say to him and he jumps off of him. Evan stands up.

"Control your mutt!" He says madly.

"Mutt? I am surprised he doesn't like you, being as you both share the same smelling breath." I respond to him sarcastically.

"Whatever, Jenna." Evan says to me as he walks away madly. Andrew and I both laugh.

"Come on, Matisse." I say as I walk up the stairs. Matisse follows me. I sit down at my computer and Matisse lies down on the carpet. My head starts to hurt and I can feel a migraine coming on. I lay my head on the desk attempting to ease it. Andrew walks into the office, and Matisse runs up to him happily. Andrew kneels, petting him.

"What's wrong, Jenna?" he asks me as he sees my head lying on the desk.

"I have a migraine." I tell him. He walks up to me and rubs my back softly.

"Do you want to go home?" he asks me. I nod.

"I'll go tell Kathleen. I'll be right back." I tell him. I lay my head on the desk. Matisse walks up to me and nudges my arm with his head.

"No Matisse, I don't feel good." I tell him. He nudges me again and I pet his head blindly. Andrew walks back into the room.

"Come on baby, let's go." He says to me. I stand up and we leave. It was already 3:00, so Andrew decided to stay home with me instead of going back to work. I lay in bed with Matisse as Andrew works on his laptop.

I drift into a deep sleep and am awoken by Matisse growling near the window in my bedroom. I walk over to it and see a man staring through my window. I scream. Andrew rushes into the room instantly.

"What's wrong?" he asks me frantically.

"There's a man out there." I tell Andrew. Andrew takes my hand in his and walks out to the living room and over to the dining room. He opens the door wall.

"Matisse. Go get him." Andrew says to Matisse. Matisse dashes out the door. Andrew and I follow him. He runs to the side of the house.

"Let me go! Let me go!" a man screams. Andrew and I run up and Matisse has his mouth around a short dark-haired slender mans wrist pulling him. I can see blood dripping down his hand.

"Come, Matisse!" I say sternly. Matisse lets go of the man and runs over to me. Andrew grabs the man by the shoulder.

"Who the hell are you?" he asks him madly.

"I'm a detective, investigating for Senator Kramer." The man's says to me.

"Investigating what?" Andrew asks him.

"For his case." The man responds. Andrew lets the man go.

"Get out of here. If you come back, I will let my dog finish you off!" Andrew tells him madly. The man nods and runs away. Andrew walks over to Matisse kneeling down.

"Good boy." Andrew tells him as he pets him. We walk back to the house and I start dinner. Eric and Matt come home, Matisse runs up to them. Eric kneels down.

"Hi Matisse." He says with a smile. Matisse licks his face. Matt walks up to me, kissing me on the cheek.

"How are you feeling, Jenna?" Matt asks me.

"Better, thank you." I tell him. I turn on the radio, and "Sara Smiles" by Hall and Oates is playing. Matt starts singing, Eric joins in. I chuckle at them as they dance around the kitchen. Eric takes my hand in his and we start dancing. Andrew smiles as he watches us.

I stir the pot and shut it off. The doorbell rings and Matt stands up.

"I got it, it's Marnie." Matt says happily. He answers the door and walks back to the table with Marnie.

"Hi Jenna." Marnie says to me.

"Hi." I respond. Matisse walks up to her, she kneels petting him.

"Awe, he's so cute. Whose dog is this?" Marnie asks me.

"He is the family dog." I tell her. She nods and stands up, walking to the dining room table sitting down. I place the dinner on the table and walk away. My head was still scrambled from my earlier migraine, I didn't even think when I did it, and, within seconds, Matisse is standing in the middle of the table eating our dinner.

"Get down!" Andrew yells to him. Matisse jumps down but it's too late; he had engulfed all of our dinner. Matisse walks over to me with his head low, knowing he did something wrong.

"That was bad, Matisse." I say to him. He whines and lies on the floor. I smile and sit down next to him, petting him. He drags his body across the floor and lays his head in my lap. Andrew laughs.

"That dog has you wrapped around his large paws." Andrew says to me.

"He's just a baby." I tell Andrew. Andrew laughs loudly.

"He weighs more than you!" He responds to me. I frown at him madly. He shakes his head. Matt stands up.

"Marnie and I will go pick up some pizzas." Matt offers. Andrew nods his head and they leave.

Chapter X

After we eat pizza, I walk to the bedroom to play on my laptop. As I lie on the bed, Matisse lies next to me. Andrew walks into the room, and sits on the bed. Matisse drags his body over to Andrew, lying his head on his lap.

"It doesn't work with me, buddy." Andrew tells him with a raised eyebrow. Matisse whines. I look sideways at Andrew and I can see he is being affected as Matisse whines. Finally, he caves in and pets him, I smile.

"We are such pushovers." Andrew says as he hugs Matisse."

"No we aren't, we just love him." I tell him. Andrew shakes his head.

"Can you imagine when we have children?" he asks me.

"Children? No I don't want any of those. I'm happy with you and Matisse. It's all I need." I tell him.

"What do you mean? You don't want to have a family with me?" he asks me.

"We have a family. We have Eric, Matt, Matisse, you and me." I tell him happily.

"Jenna you know what I mean." He says to me.

"I don't know Andrew. I don't think I would be a very good mother."

"What are you talking about? Look how you are with Matisse, you will be a fantastic mother."

"I don't know." I tell him.

"Down, Matisse." Andrew says to him. Matisse jumps off the bed, and lies down on the floor. Andrew moves closer to me, draping his arm around me. "I want to have a big family." He continues.

"What's big?" I ask him.

"At least four children, if not more." He responds happily. I shake my head.

"No way, I am not pushing out four children." I tell him.

"Yes you will."

"No I won't."

"Yes you will because you love me and want to make me happy."

"That's so wrong, using love to get your way." He kisses me softly on the lips.

"I'm an attorney, I use what is necessary." He responds, smiling. He pulls me close to him, kissing me passionately. Matisse jumps on the bed and starts licking our faces, interrupting us. We both laugh. Matisse jumps on Andrew and they start to wrestle. I stare at them and smile.

I walk out to the living room to straighten up as Andrew plays with Matisse. I finish folding a load of laundry and walk back into the bedroom. I gaze at the bed, smiling. Andrew and Matisse are asleep lying side by side. I change into a silk night shirt and slide into bed.

I was nervous about leaving Matisse home as I went to work. I hugged him ten times before Andrew pulls me out of the house. I tear up as we drive away from the house.

"He will be okay Jenna." Andrew says to me.

"What happens if he gets scared and I'm not there?" I tell him tearfully. He pulls over to the side of the road and embraces me tightly.

"Baby, he will be okay. I promise." He says as he strokes my head gently.

"I miss him already." I tell Andrew, sniffling. He kisses my head and then drives off.

It had been awhile since I had spoken to my sister. I lift my work phone and call her, but the number I remember is disconnected, then I realized Christie had called a few days ago to let me know that her number had been changed, apparently Charlie turned into a stalker and would call Christie all day and night long, to avoid another confrontation between Charlie and Manny, she just simply changed her number. I rummage through my purse and realize I had left my cell in the car. I slide my coat on and without thinking, or telling Andrew, I run out to the car.

The sun catches my attention as it shines down on me, it was a surprise. It was not normal in February for the sun to shine brightly. I walk to the car and open the door. I gaze around the car, looking for it, and then realize I had slid it into the glove compartment, I smile as I retrieve it. I slam the car door shut and walk back to the office. As I reach the end of the parking lot, I am grabbed and pulled to the side. I turn, and holding me, is Ben. I gasp.

"Let me go, Ben!" I say to him. He releases me, I turn to walk away and he grabs me again.

"Oh no, you don't. You are not going anywhere!" He says sternly. I push him.

"Leave me alone!" I tell him madly. He grabs me again.

"You are my wife."

"I am not your wife anymore, now let me go!" I scream. He places his hand over my mouth, and drags me towards his car. I kick, attempting to release his hold on me. But he is stronger and I am unsuccessful.

As we reach his car, he opens the door with one hand, holding me with the other. I bite the hand holding me, and with natural reflex he releases me. I run as fast as I can, screaming as I reach the edge of the parking lot. He jumps at me and we tumble to the ground.

"Get away from me!" I scream. He back hands me across the face.

"You are being a very bad girl!" He retorts. He stands over me and I sit up. He places his hand on his gold buckle dark brown leather belt, and slides it out of his belt loops.

The familiar burn of the belt as it hits my back makes me tremble.

"Please Ben, no!" I plead with him. He raises the belt in the air and I close my eyes as I wait for the next inevitable snap of the gold buckle dark brown leather belt. Instead, I feel arms wrap around me.

"Jenna, are you alright?" I open my eyes and Eric is kneeled beside me. I embrace him instantly.

"I'm okay." I tell him. Franklin is standing beside Ben, two security guards hold Ben in place.

"Take Jenna in, I will make sure that Ben is taken to the police." Franklin tells Eric. Eric helps me off the ground and walks me into the office. Andrew rushes down the stairs as we walk in. He walks up to me.

"Where did you go? I was just up in your office." Andrew asks me worriedly.

"I went to the car." I answer quickly. He embraces me.

"Ow!" I say as his arms graze the fresh belt mark on my back. He pulls away.

"Jenna, what's wrong with your back?" Andrew asks disconcerted. Eric approaches him.

"Ben hit her. He was in the parking lot." Eric tells him.

"What? Where is he?" Andrew asks as he rushes to the front door.

"Franklin and the security guards took him to the police." Eric answers. Andrew walks back over to me, and gently embraces me.

"Oh baby." He says distraught.

"I'm okay." I tell him.

Andrew places his hand in mine and we walk to the bathroom. He closes and locks the door then gently lifts my shirt, staring at the mark that encompassed my back. He touches it gently. I wince.

"I'm sorry." He says softly. I turn to him and stare at him, the hurt and pain in his eyes were all too familiar to me. It was the same expression I had every time Ben would hurt me. It's when I realized, that everything I now felt, he felt as well. Ben's abuse on me, was abuse for Andrew.

I place my hand gently on his face. He closes his eyes, embracing my touch. Tears fall from his eyes and I place my hand on his head, bringing his face closer to mine. I close my eyes and kiss his eyes drying his tears softly with my lips. As I stand straight up, he opens his eyes and I see his fragile heart. An instant bond ensues between us, one that no one but the two of us shared. Love, trust, loyalty; he was mine and I was his, we were one. I embrace him.

"I love you." I whisper in his ear.

"I love you." He responds emotionally. I kiss him softly.

"I'm okay, really don't worry." I say with a smile. My smile comforts him and he smiles back. I place his hand in mine and I open the door and we walk out of the bathroom.

I stare at the clock all day long, and when it hits 5:30, I rush down the stairs and I am surprised to see Andrew standing by the door, smiling and waiting for me.

"Why are you standing by the door?" I ask him.

"I knew you wanted to leave right away. Your baby's at home." He responds with a smirk. I nod my head. Andrew opens the door and I run out of the office. It seemed like the fifteen minute drive took forever. I jump out of the car before Andrew stops and rushes into the house. I open the utility door and Matisse jumps at me, we fall down to the ground and I hug him tightly. Andrew walks into the room and laughs as he watches us.

I walk over to the couch and sit down. Matisse jumps up and lays his head on my lap. I pet him as I nuzzle my face in his fur.

"Jenna." Andrew says to me. I pet Matisse staring at him.

"Yes?"

"We need to train Matisse to sleep in the utility room." He says to me. I shake my head.

"No." I respond sadly.

"Yes. He has a great bed in there, it's not being cruel." He says to me.

"Okay, but not right now, he needs us." I tell him.

"The sooner the better." He says to me. I nod my head sadly.

After dinner, Andrew places Matisse in the utility room, closing the door. I lie on the bed curled up to my pillow, tears fall down my face. Andrew walks into the room and undresses down to his boxers and slides in next to me, wrapping his arms around me.

"I know your upset, but he has to learn to sleep by himself." Andrew tells me.

"It's so mean." I tell him, sobbing. He turns me facing him.

"Oh baby, don't cry." He says as he embraces me tightly.

"I know he's scared. He's all alone Andrew." I respond, sobbing harder. He wipes my tears from my face and exhales. He kisses me quickly on the lips and stands up, sliding his pants on and leaves the room. I sit, waiting for him. Matisse leaps on the bed and my heart fills with joy. I hug him tightly.

"Matisse!" I say aloud kissing him and hugging him. Andrew smiles as he slides back into bed. I move to the middle of the bed and I embrace Andrew tightly.

"Thank you." I say to him.

"This is only temporary. I really want to teach him to sleep in the utility room." Andrew tells me sternly.

"Why can't he sleep in the spare room? I think I will feel better if he has his own room with his own bed, the utility room is so cold and dark." I say to him. Andrew chuckles.

"You want to put a dog in a real bed, with his own bedroom?" He questions me. I nod my head. He exhales again.

"I'll try anything at this point." He says to me. I hug him tightly.

For the next few nights, we put Matisse in his own bedroom and he adjusts to the bed quickly. Andrew is happy to have our bedroom all to ourselves again.

I walk out to the living room, and Andrew is sitting on the couch gazing through paper work. I plop next to him, and he drapes his arm around me.

"Morning, baby." He says softly.

"Morning." I tell him.

Today was court day, so Andrew was looking through all the paperwork, making sure everything was in check. Being as I had an annulment, I had to take back my maiden name: Dotson. Andrew wanted to make sure that my last name was changed in every box. He wanted no excuse to delay this court date.

Andrew was already showered and ready, so I went into the bathroom and took a shower and dressed.

The courthouse was busy as Andrew and I walked to the door, we are attacked instantly by the media. Andrew hovers over me and pushes through them into the courthouse. I was not testifying. William felt they had enough evidence to win the case, which brought Andrew great relief. Andrew wanted to keep Ben as far away from me as he could.

Andrew and I decide to wait outside the court room for William and the prosecutor. It takes hours until William finally walks out the courtroom.

"They found him guilty of felonious assault and stalking." William says proudly. I stand, hugging him. Finally, we had our day in court, and Ben would pay for what he had done to me.

"Thank you." I tell him.

"You're so welcomed." William responds. I embrace Andrew. William gestures to Andrew.

"I'm going to go talk to my father, I'll be right back." He tells me. I nod my head.

The court room door flies open and Ben walks out, smiling with his attorney. I look down, wishing I could disappear. He notices me and walks over. I stand up.

"How are you?" Ben asks me nicely.

"I'm good." I tell him. He places his hands on my shoulder. I shudder at his touch.

"I miss you, Jenna." He says to me. I pull away from him.

"Leave me alone, Ben." I tell him. My reaction does not faze him. He walks closer to me, placing his hands on my back. He lifts my shirt and slides his hands until he reaches the branding he had given me.

"Your mine Jenna, always mine." He whispers as he slides his finger slowly across the branding.

"Get your hands off of her!" Andrew screams as he runs up. Ben backs up. Security guards instantly surround us. They grab Andrew. Ben laughs at him.

"I cannot have a civil conversation with my ex-wife?" Ben asks with a chuckle.

"There is nothing civil about you, you're a woman beater. You stay away from her."

"She's mine Andrew. When are you going to get that through your head? No matter what you do. She will always belong to me."

"No that's where you're wrong. She doesn't love you, she loves me. It kills you, because you know deep down inside that what I say is true." Andrew says to him, gritting his teeth.

The smile instantly leaves Bens face as Andrew's words affect him. He looks confused and lost. I stand and walk over to Andrew; he drapes his arm around me as he still glares at Ben.

"Come on baby, let's go home." He turns and we walk away.

Ben was on bond as he awaiting sentencing. Andrew and I drive home and take Matisse for a walk. I place my arm in his as he holds Matisse's leash.

"My mother is in town. She really wants to come over, she has something for you." Andrew says to me.

"Okay. When does she want to come over?" I ask him.

"I told her after dinner."

"That works for me."

"Now that court is over. I would really like to move on with our lives."

"Okay. I agree."

"I want to start planning our wedding."

I don't reply.

"Jenna?" Andrew asks me worriedly.

"Andrew, you know what I just realized? I don't even know how old you are."

"I'm 26." He responds.

"I don't know your middle name."

"Thomas."

"Mine's Louise." I respond proudly. Andrew smiles.

"I like that. So do you still want to marry me, Louise?" He asks me cutely. I stop and turn to face him.

"Yes, yes and yes!" I respond to him. He embraces me tightly. We walk down to the park and let Matisse off of the leash. He immediately runs into the lake. I become nervous as he struggles to swim. I run without thinking into the cold water and grab him.

"Jenna! You're going to get sick! It's too cold to be in the lake!" He screams to me. I walk up to Andrew, soaking wet from head to toe, shivering. He takes his jacket off and places it around me, then attaches the leash to Matisse and we walk home. It was the middle of February and only 35 degrees out. I felt like a Popsicle by the time we reach the house. Andrew puts Matisse in the utility room to dry off then takes me into the bedroom. I strip off all of my clothes and jump into the bed, covering up with the blankets. Andrew strips down to his boxers and crawls in next to me.

"Come here, baby." He says to me with his arms wide open. I cuddle close to his chest and he wraps his arms around me tightly. It doesn't take long before my body begins to warm up.

"Why did you jump in the lake?" He asks me in a scolding voice.

"I thought Matisse was drowning." I tell him.

"He's a dog. They can swim." He says to me.

"I know that now, I didn't know that then." I tell him.

I fall asleep, Andrew calls his mother and reschedules for her to come the next day.

I wake in the middle of the night, sneezing. I felt hot, and sweat is beading on my forehead. Andrew sits up sleepily.

"What's wrong?" Andrew asks me.

"I don't feel good." I tell him. He touches my forehead.

"You're burning up." He says to me worriedly.

"I think it's just the flu." I tell him. He jumps out of bed and walks to the bathroom and grabs some ibuprofen, then grabs a water bottle off the nightstand. I take the pills and lie back down. He strokes my head gently.

"Try to sleep." He says to me. I nod my head and lay back down.

I wake in the morning, sneezing and feverish. My nose is dripping and filling faster than I can blow it. Andrew walks into the bedroom from the bathroom. He looks at me worriedly as he sits down on the bed.

"Maybe I should stay home with you, you look terrible." He says to me. I shake my head.

"No, go to work. It's just the flu." I tell him.

"Okay, I will get home as I can." He says to me. I nod my head. He smiles at me as he sees my red nose and watery eyes.

"You look so pathetic right now." He says with a slight smile.

"I feel terrible." I tell him. He kisses me on the forehead.

"Oh baby, I wish I could take it away." He embraces me.

"I wish you could too." I say to him. He lays me on the pillow.

"I'll be home soon, sleep." He tells me. I nod my head and curl to the pillow. He stands up and leaves.

I sleep all day long.

I am awoken by Andrew when he arrives home from work. I sit up sleepily.

"Here baby, take this, your still running a fever." He says handing me ibuprofen. I take the pills and lie back down. He strokes my head gently. "Are you sure you don't want to go to the doctors?" he asks me. I shake my head.

"It's just the flu." I tell him. He slides next to me, wrapping his arms around me. I turn to him. "You might not want to lie next to me you could catch it." I tell him softly. He cuddles close to me.

"Then I catch it. I'm not ever sleeping without you." He tells me. I smile, closing my eyes.

I wake in the morning and I am worse, coughing and sneezing. And my fever is higher. Andrew takes the thermometer from my ear.

"I'm taking you to the hospital." He says sternly.

"No. I don't want to go to the hospital." I tell him stubbornly.

"Too bad. Your fever is too high and you're not getting any better." He says worriedly.

Andrew helps me dress because I am too weak to lift my arms. After I dress, he places his arm around me and drives me to the hospital. He calls his father, letting him know what he was doing. We walk into the emergency room and they take us back right away. They take my blood, and x-rays of my lungs, and admit me. It was pneumonia, I was dehydrated and they needed to give me antibiotics through an IV and fluids to rehydrate me. I am not happy as they place me in the bed in my room. Andrew laughs as I sit in the bed pouting.

"There is no reason to pout. You are sick."

"I know." I respond, frowning. He snickers at my reaction. His cell rings and he answers it.

"Yeah… no, the third floor… Okay, I'll be right down." He hangs up his cell and stands.

"I have to go get Manny and Christie, they can't find the room." He tells me. I nod my head. He kisses my forehead and leaves. I turn on the television and flip through the five available stations.

"Jenna." I turn and Ben is walking up to my bed. Fear fills me instantly.

"What are you doing here?" I ask him nervously. He sits on the chair next to my bed.

"You're sick. I wanted to make sure you were okay." He tells me.

"Ben, you shouldn't be here." I say to him frantically.

"Why not? Because your boyfriend will be upset? You are mine and will always be mine. I don't care what he says." He explains to me.

"You better care." Andrew states as he walks into the room. Christie and Manny walk in behind him. Ben stands up.

"I can't visit my ex-wife when she is sick?" Ben asks him. Andrew walks closer to him.

"No! Now get the hell out of here before I lose my manners." Andrew tells him with infuriation.

"Are you threatening me?" Ben asks him.

"I can't do this anymore." Andrew says, shaking his head. Without warning, he clenches his fist and punches Ben in the face, knocking him to the ground.

"No Andrew, don't!" I plead with him. Manny walks over to me.

"Let him be Jenna. He needs to get it out." Manny tells me. Andrew kneels down and starts punching Ben relentlessly in the face.

"How does it feel, how does it fucking feel to be so helpless!" Andrew screams as he continues his beating on Ben.

Security guards rush into the room, pulling Andrew off of Ben, detaining him. Ben stands up; blood is oozing from his nose and mouth. He takes a handkerchief out, gently wiping the blood from his face.

"You are going to regret doing that!" Ben says to Andrew with a sneer.

"Get the hell out of here!" Andrew screams. Ben leaves and the security guards release Andrew. He walks over to my bed, Manny moves aside, letting him sit down on the chair next to the bed.

"Andrew, did you have to hurt him so bad?" I ask him.

"Did he have to hurt you so bad? I didn't hurt him half as bad as he hurt you." He stands up.

"Scoot over." He says to me. He lies next to me, stroking my head gently.

"I will always protect you. I promised you I would never let him hurt you again and I plan on keeping that promise. I love you, you are everything to me." He says with endearment.

"I wish I could kiss you right now." I respond tearfully.

"Why can't you?" he asks me.

"Cause I" —Andrew interrupts me, placing his lips to mine. After we finish kissing I stare into his eyes.

"I love you." I say as I smile at him.

"I love you more." He responds. He wraps his arms around me cuddling me close.

They released me the next day.

Andrew went to play hockey with Manny for the day. I sit with Matisse in the living room lounging. He walks to the door wall, whining. I open it and let him out, then sit back down on the couch. I gaze through a magazine for awhile and stare up at the door wall.

Normally, Matisse would only stay outside long enough to use the bathroom and come back up to the door wall. I give him a few more minutes then walk to the door wall calling his name.

"Matisse!" I scream. I stand, gazing around the yard and can't find him. I decide to walk to the side of the house. I turn, and what I see freezes me in my tracks. I scream, my body shakes and I fall to the ground as I see Matisse's lifeless body stretched out across the grass. I hug him.

"Matisse!" I sob. Eric and Matt run up as I sit up and look at my hands and shirt, and they are full of blood. Matt grabs me, embracing me tightly.

"Please help him! Please help him!" I plead, sobbing. Eric and Matt gently pick him up and carry him to the car, as I follow. They place him in the back and I sit next to him, petting his head and holding him.

"Matisse!" I say sobbing. Eric and Matt rush Matisse into the veterinary hospital and they take him back right away. I sit, staring at his blood all over me, crying. Eric holds me close.

The veterinarian informs me that he has a broken leg that required surgery. I wait, sobbing.

Andrew rushes into the veterinary hospital, he immediately runs up to me, embracing me tightly.

"Oh baby." He says distraught.

"He's hurt, Andrew, he's hurt so bad." I tell him. He cradles me in his arm, rocking me lightly.

"He will be okay Jenna. He's strong; I promise he will be okay." He explains to me.

We wait for two hours, when the veterinarian walks out, I stand up and rush to him, with Andrew by my side.

"How is he?" I ask the vet.

"He's good. The surgery went well. He had a few cuts that we had to suture, but he will make a full recovery." He explains to me. I exhale with relief, I embrace Andrew tightly.

"Thank you doctor." I say to him relieved.

"I want to show you something." He says to us. We nod and follow him to the back. Matisse is still sleeping on the table as we walk up. The vet looks up at us he points to Matisse's back. I move closer to it.

"You know branding is illegal on a household pet?" The vet says to us madly. Andrew and I stare at his back. We see the words MINE branded. I gasp and begin to tremble.

"We didn't do that." Andrew tells the vet. My breathing becomes sparse. I place my hands on my knees, bending. Andrew looks down at me worriedly.

"Breathe, Jenna." He says to me. I can't catch my breath, I can't think. I look up at Andrew and the room starts to spin, I fall to the ground, passing out.

I wake lying on a couch. I sit up, rubbing my head. Andrew rubs my back lightly. I turn to him.

"Ben branded him." I say to him, sobbing. He nods and embraces me.

"I know. Don't worry Jenna, I called detective Mason, they picked him up about a half hour ago." Andrew tells me.

"He's never going to stop. Until he hurts everyone and everything I love." I say to him, disconcerted.

"No baby, don't think like that." He says to me.

Matisse had to stay in the hospital for a few days, so Andrew and I leave and drive home.

The house felt empty without Matisse. I missed him so much. Andrew sits next to me on the couch, draping his arm around me.

"I was thinking maybe if you're okay with it, we could get married in New York. What do you think about that?" Andrew asks me.

"I don't care, whatever you want." I say, shrugging my shoulders, staring at the ground.

"I was thinking we could have an outdoor reception."

"Okay, whatever you want."

"I was also thinking about hooking up with Kelly again."

"Okay, whatever you want." He places his hands on my shoulders, turning me to face him.

"Jenna, you are not paying attention to anything I am saying to you."

"I'm sorry. I'm just thinking about Matisse and what Ben did to him."

"You can't change what he did to Matisse, so stop thinking about it so much. I want to talk about our wedding." He says to me, pouting. His pouty lips bring a smile to my face. I stroke his cheek gently.

"I'm sorry, honey." I tell him with a giggle.

"No you're not." He responds, still pouting. I crawl onto his lap, and he smiles, wrapping his arms around me.

"I should pout more often." He says, smiling. He places his lips to mine. Our kisses become passionate quickly. He scoops me into his arms and carries me to the bedroom, laying me on the bed. He sits me up and slides my shirt off, then kisses me as he unclasps my bra. He slides my blue jeans and panties off then lies on top of me. He cups my breast in his hands as he kisses me gently. I turn him over, never letting my lips leave his. I slide his shirt off, and then I kiss his chest moving my way down to his stomach. I kiss his stomach and he moans loudly. I unbutton his pants and slide them off with his boxers. I then take him in my hand.

"Oh!" he moans as I stroke him gently. I move and take him in my mouth. He places his hands on my head gently as his hips gyrate in sync with my mouth.

"Oh, Jenna!" He moans. His hips move faster as he reaches his peak. I take a deep breath as he releases in my mouth. I crawl up his body and he smiles at me.

"You are a remarkable woman." he says with a smirk. He places his lips to mine, kissing me passionately. I am aroused instantly. I sit up on him and put him inside of me. I move up and down on him slowly. He sits up, cupping my breasts, suckling my nipples. I moan loudly as I begin to climb. He places his hands on my hips, moving me up and down faster on him.

"Andrew!" I scream as I reach my peak. Two quick strokes and he follows. I fall on his chest, exhausted. He rubs my back gently. My thighs shake as I move from atop of him, sliding next to him. He brushes the hair back from my forehead smiling as he stares into my eyes.

"I love you."

"I love you too."

Andrew and I wake early in the morning. It was Ben's sentencing day, and Andrew insisted on being there to make sure that Ben paid the price for all that he had done to us.

The media covered the front of the courthouse. Detective Mason guided us to the back so bad, to avoid them. We wait outside the courtroom for William and the prosecutor. It takes only a half hour before they walk out. I could tell instantly by the expression on

William's face it was not good news. Andrew and I stand as he walks over to us.

"The judge sentenced him to 5 years probation." William says to us. I gasp, shaking my head.

"What the hell? How can that be possible?" Andrew asks enraged. The prosecutor walks up to us.

"Did he pay you off?" Andrew asks the prosecutor.

"Andrew, they changed judges on us at sentencing, obviously the new judge is a friend of Bens."

"How the hell can they give him probation? Everything he did to us, everything he continues to do to us. He branded our dog. Isn't there some law against that?" Andrew screams.

"They found that inadmissible from lack of evidence." Andrew paces back and forth angrily.

"Lack of evidence? Our dog has the words MINE branded into his back! Tell me how the hell there is lack of evidence!" Andrew screams.

"I'm sorry Andrew I really am." The prosecutor states as he walks away hurriedly.

The court doors open, and Ben walks out laughing. He smiles as he sees me. He walks over to us; Andrew places me behind him protectively.

"Hi darling." He says to me.

"She's not your darling." Andrew says with a sneer.

"She will always be my darling. She will always be mine." He retorts. Andrew glares at him.

"When are you going to give up Andrew? You will never beat me." Ben says with a chuckle. Andrew exhales, looking down at the ground. As he lifts his head he smiles at Ben.

"I already have." Andrew says to Ben calmly.

"What are you talking about?" Ben asks him.

"With your power and money, you can have anyone and anything, but you can't have her, can you? And it devastates you to be so powerless. You don't think I don't know what it's like to want her? I've been there. She's an addiction, a need so deep nothing else matters but her. You think about her, even when she is standing right in front of you. You can't breathe unless you're near her. She is everything, isn't she Ben? Everything, that is, but yours. She is not yours anymore, and never will be again. I have showed her a life of love, attention, compassion, and understanding, something you never bothered to do. She loves me, I am hers and she is mine… not yours, Ben, mine." Andrew says to him softly. He turns, smiling at me. Tears fills my eyes as his words touch my heart deeply, he touches my face, softly comforting me.

Ben stands distraught and shaken as Andrew's words leave him speechless. Andrew places his hand in mine and we leave.

We drive home and Andrew places his hand in mine.

"I have a surprise for you." He says with a smile.

"What is it?" I ask him.

"If I told you, it wouldn't be a surprise." He responds. He pulls up in the driveway. I step out of the car and Andrew walks over to me, taking my hand. I walk into the house and he walks me into Matisse's bedroom. Matisse is lying on the bed. Excitement fills me and I rush to the bed, gently hugging Matisse.

"Matisse, I missed you so much!" I say as I rest my head gently on him. He lifts his head and licks my face. I slide onto the bed next to him and gently pet him. Andrew stands by the door, smiling.

I was happy to have Matisse home again. Andrew and I hired a young girl to take care of Matisse while we worked. She arrives on time. I kiss and hug Matisse and we leave for work.

Andrew is driving down the road when he grabs his stomach.

"What's wrong?" I ask him.

"I don't know." He responds to me.

"Did you eat something bad this morning?"

"No. It's the pain I get when something bad is going to happen. I'm taking you home." He continues. He does a U-turn and drives back to the house.

"Andrew, I have to go to work."

"Not today baby." He pulls into the driveway and walks me into the house.

"I want you to lock the doors and don't let anyone in."

"Okay."

"I'm going to work, to set up Eric and Matt, and I will be back as quickly as I can."

"Okay." He embraces me.

"I love you Jenna."

"I love you too." I send the dog sitter home. I walk into Matisse's room checking on him, and he is sound asleep. I close his door and quietly walk over to the couch sitting down. I grasp a magazine and gaze through it. I hear the door wall quietly open and close. I stand up and walk over to it, and Ben is standing there. I am instantly terrified.

"Did you miss me, darling?" he asks with a wicked grin. I attempt to run away from him, but he pounces on me, knocking me on the ground. I sit up and slowly use my legs to scoot away from him. He smiles at me.

"You are not going anywhere!" He says as he grabs my ankles, pulling me to him. He stands up.

"You better get out of here! Andrew will be back any minute!" I say to him with desperation.

"He's not coming back Jenna, I know it and you know it… You have been a very bad girl." He continues. He places his hand on his gold buckle dark brown leather belt and undoes it. I close my eyes.

I hear the front door open. I open my eyes and turn towards the front door. Andrew runs in, followed by Eric and Matt. Ben looks up at him, and Andrew smiles.

"Looks like you came on the wrong day." Andrew says to him with a wicked grin. He rushes up to him, and with his clenched fist, he hits Ben, knocking him to the ground. Eric picks me up and holds me protectively. Andrew kneels down and relentlessly punches Ben in the face and head.

"I hate you! I fucking hate you! You will never hurt her again! Do you hear me!" Andrew screams angrily as he continues to beat the living daylights out of Ben.

"He's going to kill him… he's going to kill him! Stop him, please, stop him!" I plead with Eric frantically as I pull on his shirt collar. Eric and Matt rush over to Andrew and pull him off of Ben.

"Stop Andrew, you're going to kill him!" Eric says to him as he restrains him. I stare at Andrew, his expression is crazed and confused. He attempts to pull away from Eric and Matt, wanting Ben badly.

"He deserves to die for what he did to her!" Andrew screams hoarsely.

Andrew had called the police on his way home, his gut feeling told him to. They show up and rush into the house. Detective Mason walks over to Ben, picking him up.

"What happened to you? You look like a truck hit you." Detective Mason says with a sarcastic chuckle.

Andrew walks over to me, embracing me tightly.

"Are you okay?" Andrew asks me. I nod.

I stare over at Ben. Bruises encompass his whole face, blood drips endlessly from his nose and mouth. He tilts his eyes up, and a wicked grin fills his face.

My heart starts to beat quickly as I watch Ben reach into Detective Masons holster, retrieving his gun. My breath quickens as he points it at Andrew's back.

"She is mine! Forever… Forever!" Ben screams. Without hesitation, I twirl Andrew around, using my body to shield him.

I didn't hear it, but I felt it as it entered my back. It felt like a sledge hammer hitting me at full force, pushing me forward.

Everything is instantly still, silent. So silent I can hear the whisper of my breath and the slowing beat of my heart. My mind wanders to the cliff, the waves roar angrily to the shore as the wind blows briskly. I stare up at the clear blue sky, smiling as I inhale the fresh air.

My eyes flutter as I await the light, the one they always preached you saw before you died. But, I never saw the light; all I saw was darkness…

Made in the USA
Charleston, SC
09 May 2014